One in particular ... ew that voice. She leaned ... red out, feeling like a teenage girl spying on boys.

Kirsten and Erik stood in the hallway talking to another man whose back was to Jazmyn's office. He reminded her of someone she knew.

"Just wait until he turns around," Maddy whispered in her ear.

As if he'd heard, the man turned to glance at her office. Maddy eased the door closed, but not before Jazmyn got a good look at his face. The man talking to Kirsten and Erik was Thor. Her Thor.

"Maddy, that's not the owner of this company. He's the friend of my brother's that I had lunch with."

Maddy's eyes widened. "I'm telling you he is the head of this place. Kirsten introduced me to him just before I came in here."

The air in the room congealed around Jazmyn. She had trouble breathing. Thor was not the owner. He was a simple hunting guide. He wouldn't have lied to her.

The door to her office swung open. Thor faced her with Kirsten and Erik at his back.

NANCY J. FARRIER, resides in Arizona. She is married and the mother of one son and four daughters. She is the author of numerous articles, short stories, and novels. She home-schools her three youngest daughters and writes in the evenings. Nancy enjoys sharing her faith through her writing.

Books by Nancy J. Farrier

HEARTSONG PRESENTS
HP415—Sonoran Sunrise
HP449—An Ostrich a Day
HP480—Sonoran Star
HP488—Sonoran Sweetheart
HP503—Sonoran Secret
HP528—Precious Jewels

Don't miss out on any of our super romances. Write to us at the following address for information on our newest releases and club information.

Heartsong Presents Readers' Service
PO Box 719
Uhrichsville, OH 44683

Or visit www.heartsongpresents.com

Picture
Imperfect

Nancy J. Farrier

Heartsong Presents

Thanks to my husband, John, and all the Farrier clan who gave me such a love of camping in the White Mountains of Arizona. Also, thanks to Xena, the real-life squirrel, who fought so valiantly for those chocolate bars.

A note from the Author:
I love to hear from my readers! You may correspond with me by writing:

Nancy J. Farrier
Author Relations
PO Box 719
Uhrichsville, OH 44683

ISBN 1-59310-122-8

PICTURE IMPERFECT

Copyright © 2004 by Nancy J. Farrier. All rights reserved. Except for use in any review, the reproduction or utilization of this work in whole or in part in any form by any electronic, mechanical, or other means, now known or hereafter invented, is forbidden without the permission of Heartsong Presents, an imprint of Barbour Publishing, Inc., PO Box 719, Uhrichsville, Ohio 44683.

Our mission is to publish and distribute inspirational products offering exceptional value and biblical encouragement to the masses.

All Scripture quotations are taken from the King James Version of the Bible.

All of the characters and events in this book are fictitious. Any resemblance to actual persons, living or dead, or to actual events is purely coincidental.

PRINTED IN THE U.S.A.

Or check out our Web site at www.heartsongpresents.com

one

"Jason, there are clouds lower than we are." Looking out the window, Jazmyn Rondell tried to drag her gaze from the steep drop-off on her side of her brother's SUV. Opening her mouth, she sucked in a deep draught of air, hoping to quell the nausea twisting her stomach.

"Don't you dare throw up in my new Explorer, Sis," Jason said.

"If this stupid seat belt wasn't so tight, I could curl up with my head between my knees."

Jason chuckled. "I don't remember that helping when we were kids."

"At least I wouldn't have to watch when we drop into this bottomless pit." Jazmyn took another deep breath. "You tricked me into this, Jason."

"I didn't trick you. I told you the truth."

"Right. You said you needed to find a guide for your photography expedition. You didn't say we would have to drive up Mount Everest to find him. Couldn't you have picked someone easier to locate?"

"Thor Larson is the best. I wouldn't settle for less. The layout for this next book has to be spectacular."

"So why didn't you just call on the phone like a normal person would?"

"He doesn't have a phone."

Jazmyn swung around to face her brother. "What! No phone? He lives high enough to have jet pilots wave when they fly past, yet he has no way of communicating with anyone?

What else should I know about him?"

Jason shrugged. "He's sort of a recluse. From what I've been told he keeps to himself except during hunting season when he guides hunters."

The SUV hit a deep rut, bouncing Jazmyn's head against the window. She forced herself to keep from checking to see how close they'd come to the edge of the precipice. She wouldn't admit it to Jason, but she would do just about anything for him, even climb Mount Everest.

"Jaz, I'm going to have a permanent record that you've ridden in my car."

"I'm doing my best not to throw up, Jason."

He laughed. "I'm talking about the fingers you're digging into the upholstery. They won't even have to use dust to see the prints."

"If we weren't trying to drive up this mountain goat track you insist is a road, I wouldn't have to hold on so tight."

"Lighten up, now; we're almost there. Besides, I know what's good for you."

"Yeah, right," Jazmyn muttered.

"I happen to be your twin," Jason reminded her. "Even if we didn't grow up in the same house, I know when you're miserable. Since Adam died you've shut yourself away from the world. You need some time out, and you promised to accompany me on my next photography shoot."

Pressing her lips tightly together, Jazmyn fought a wave of emotion. Adam, the only man other than Jason she'd ever trusted, had died in a fiery car crash twenty-one months and three days ago, one week before their wedding. From the age of eight, when her parents divorced and Jason left to live with their dad, Jazmyn had been virtually shut off from the world except for her mother. The year they turned nineteen, she and Jason got together again when he began to attend college in the city where she lived. Adam, Jason's friend, quickly became a major part of Jazmyn's life.

Jazmyn pushed away the memories. "Why couldn't this be like the last book where you took pictures of the kids playing at the park? Or better yet, shots of some tropical paradise?"

"Because that's not what the editor wants, and I shoot what he wants. Besides, you need some fresh mountain air. You're as pale as a ghost. The only sunlight you've seen lately is the kind filtered through the kitchen window. This will be an adventure for you."

"I don't need an adventure. I need to have my head examined for trusting you. We're exact opposites. How could you possibly know what's good for me? We may be twins, but I think they found you under a different cabbage plant."

The SUV tilted. Jazmyn felt the seat belt tighten, holding her in place. She pointedly looked away from the drop-off and up the hill on the driver's side of the gleaming black Explorer. "Jason, watch out!"

Jason hit the brakes, halting their already slow progress. "What?"

"He has a gun."

Jason leaned forward and peered up the hill. "Who?"

"A man. He had this huge gun. He was staring at me like he wanted to shoot." She reached out and clenched Jason's arm. "What if this was a warning?"

"Relax." Jason grinned. "Maybe he was a mirage."

"Jason, you don't have mirages in the mountains. I know he was real. He had these piercing eyes. He glared at me."

"Glared at you?" Jason leaned back and laughed. Jazmyn folded her arms across her chest, biting her lip to keep from yelling. Jason could laugh all he wanted, but she knew that man hadn't wanted them here. The way he stared at her, even for just an instant, sent a shiver down her spine.

Wrapping his hand around the gearshift, Jason put the SUV into first. "I know you get scared, but this is paranoid. You've got to start trusting God with your fears."

Gritting her teeth, Jazmyn forced her eyes back to the narrow track in front of them. "Stop." Her palm slapped the dashboard. "We can't go on. The road isn't there." She gasped as she looked closer at the deep cut washed out in the road. During a rainstorm this would be a waterfall shooting down into the valley below. Now dry, the bank rose up on Jason's side of the vehicle. The drop-off on Jazmyn's side split apart by more than two feet.

Jason revved the engine.

"What are you doing?"

He grinned as he put the SUV in gear. "Living dangerously."

"Jason!" Jazmyn yelped. She reached for the door handle and then felt the blood drain from her face as she realized the first step would be a long one.

Slowly the SUV edged close to the bank, the tires on the left side going up onto the hill. The Explorer tilted. Jazmyn squeezed her eyes shut. *God, why did I agree to come? My brother is crazy.* She waited for her life to flash before her eyes. Isn't that what people always claimed happened when they were close to death?

"Jaz, you can breathe again."

She squinted through one eye to see Jason grinning at her. Opening her eyes, she saw that the Explorer rested on all four tires, the washed-out road behind them. She gave a sigh of relief. "That was really foolish," she snapped. "What if we had gone over the edge?"

Jason chuckled. "At least I got some color in your cheeks."

Biting her lip to stop a smile, Jazmyn turned away. From the time they were toddlers until their parents' divorce, Jason had been dragging her into one adventure after another. Each time she had wanted to be furious but found she couldn't resist his impish grin. She couldn't stay mad at him.

Twenty minutes later, Jason rounded a sharp curve in the road and pulled to a stop. "We're here."

Jazmyn groaned. The cabin facing them looked like a slightly more modern version of an 1800s shack. A wooden porch stretched along the front, the weathered boards in desperate need of painting. Metal traps of various sizes hung from pegs along the walls, their sharp teeth grinning as if eager for a kill. A forest of pine and evergreen stood sentinel around the perimeter. In defiance of the building's aged look, a glossy dark green Ford truck rested under the trees to the left of the cabin.

"Jason." Jazmyn's whisper broke the silence. "What are we doing here?"

"Relax." He shut off the engine. Total silence rushed over them. "I can't wait to meet Thor. I hear he's a great hunter."

"I can just imagine. With a name like that he's probably some Norse god with a hammer in one hand and a lightning bolt in the other."

Jason laughed and opened his door. "I've heard some fantastic stories about him but never anything like that."

Stepping out into the cool mountain air, Jazmyn shivered.

"Cold?" Jason asked.

"Terrified would be more accurate. I didn't even notice the temperature." She wanted to throw something when Jason laughed at her comment. "Look, brother dear, I don't think anyone is home. Let's leave. Maybe you can find another editor to work for."

"Not a chance." Jason headed toward the cabin. "I've waited too long for an opportunity like this one."

They were nearing the porch when a pack of wild-eyed, sharp-toothed beasts rounded the corner and enveloped them.

Jazmyn opened her mouth to scream. Nothing came out. She closed her eyes, certain they would be torn to pieces. Never had she seen such fierce animals.

"Loki, Odin!" The rough command echoed in the clearing.

Jason's hand squeezed her arm. She eased her eyes open enough to see that what she had assumed to be a dozen savage brutes were actually two dogs standing before her, their tongues lolling. No doubt they were savoring an image of her with an apple stuffed in her mouth.

Looking beyond the dogs, she gasped. *It's him,* she wanted to whisper to Jason. *He's the man I saw in the woods.* But the words stuck in her throat. She grabbed the back of Jason's shirt and leaned closer to him. The huge man at the corner of the cabin pierced her with an electric blue gaze. Hanks of white-gold hair stuck out at odd angles beneath the dark blue hunter's cap he wore. His mouth made a straight line over a clenched jaw. She tried to ignore the broad shoulders and muscular build. She didn't want to acknowledge the strange excitement that raced through her when he held her with his gaze. He looked like her idea of a Norse god. The sleeves of his flannel shirt were rolled back from his wrists to reveal muscular forearms. Time stood still when she lowered her gaze to his hands.

Jazmyn inched closer to Jason until her nose touched the fabric of his shirt. *He's just murdered someone.* Fear constricted her throat. She couldn't take her eyes from the long-bladed, bloody knife he held in his left hand.

"Thor Larson?" Jason's question startled her. He stepped toward the killer, holding out his hand, ignoring the growling dogs.

"Jason, stop." Her voice ended in a frightened squeak.

He ignored her. "I'm Jason Rondell. This is my sister, Jazmyn. I'm looking for a guide. I've been told you're the best."

Thor lifted his right hand toward Jason's outstretched palm. The carcasses of two rabbits dangled limply from his fingers. Bile burned in Jazmyn's throat. Black dots danced across her vision. *Oh, God, don't let me faint. Please get us out of here.*

In one deft movement, Thor transferred the murder victims to the hand with the knife. He shook Jason's hand, causing her brother to wince.

"I'm afraid you're mistaken, Mr. Rondell. I only guide during the hunting season. If you want to poach animals, you'll have to find someone else. Now, if you'll excuse me." Thor turned toward the cabin.

"Mr. Larson."

Thor turned back, one foot on the bottom porch step.

"I don't want to kill any animals. I'm a photographer. I need to do a layout for a book. It's an important shoot for me. I need a guide. I know you're the best, and I'm willing to pay well."

Jazmyn didn't understand how Jason could so calmly face a man who almost dwarfed him in size. Thor looked like he could wrestle a bear. For all she knew he did that as part of his daily routine. She breathed a sigh of relief that it wasn't her those brilliant blue eyes were boring into.

&

City slickers, Thor thought. *Why do they always come looking for me?* He raised his arm, rubbing his sleeve against his chin. The faint rasp of the stubble reminded him he hadn't shaved today. He studied Jason Rondell, wanting to say no, but something held him back. His gaze strayed to Jazmyn peeking out from behind her brother. Her wide eyes and tense stance reminded him of a deer caught in headlights moments before it bolted into the woods.

"Come on in." He gestured to the door. "I need to get these rabbits on to soak. Then we can talk."

Jason climbed the steps with Jazmyn doing her best to stay

close to him. Thor fought back a grin as he watched her pale complexion turn white. She watched his hunting knife with a look of dread until she came abreast of him. Glancing up, she turned pink as she caught him watching her.

Thor strode through the door after the Rondells. "In there." He nodded toward the small sofa in the sitting area. "I'll only be a few minutes." Dangling the rabbits by their ears, he went onto the back porch where he had a sink installed for cleaning game.

Within five minutes Thor had the two rabbits skinned and soaking in salt water. He scrubbed his hands and took a minute to slick his hair into a semblance of order. He rubbed a hand over his stubbly chin, then shook his head. What did he care if he wasn't clean-shaven? He didn't want to impress anyone.

In his mind he could still see Jazmyn standing outside his cabin. She'd been terrified of his dogs, despite the fact they would rather lick people to death than bite them. The sun had glinted off the red-gold highlights in her hair, which hung in a mass of curls. Thor gave himself a mental shake, forcing the vision of her delicate features from his mind. He refused to be attracted to any woman. Never again would he allow a woman to get close to him. He knew he had to protect himself, and his secret, from all women. He would simply concentrate on playing the part of the backwoods hunting guide.

Thor stepped inside and strode into the sitting area. Jason stood at the far wall admiring the large elk head hanging there. Jazmyn huddled on the couch looking like a whipped puppy—utterly adorable.

"How can I help you, Mr. Rondell?"

"Please, call me Jason." The young man turned to face him, a personable smile lighting his handsome features. He ran a hand over his short-cropped reddish-brown curls. "As I said,

I'm a photographer. My editor wants me to do a layout for a book on wildlife in the White Mountains. I need someone who is familiar with the area and can get me the best shots."

"When?"

"As soon as possible. I'll need a couple of weeks' notice to get all my equipment ready."

Thor nodded and glanced over at Jazmyn. Leaning forward on the sofa, she held out her hand, trying to entice the old dog curled up in the corner to come to her. Her lips were pursed as she made soft kissing sounds. The dog slept on.

"It won't work." He could see he'd startled her. She looked up at him, frozen in place, her hand still outstretched.

"That's Frey," he said. "He was my first hunting dog. When he died I couldn't bear to part with him. Since I also do taxidermy, I stuffed him and kept him around."

A look of horror crossed Jazmyn's face.

two

"You stuffed your dog?" Jazmyn's voice squeaked as she snatched her hand back into her lap.

Thor gave a slow grin that reminded her of Jason's impish smiles. "It's kind of like Roy Rogers and his horse Trigger. I wanted to keep Frey around for the memories. He and I had a lot of good times together."

Jazmyn shuddered. What other dark secrets did this man have? What about people he loved? If they died, did he stuff them so he could keep alive the fond memories? And just what did he do with those who gave him bad memories? Visions of the bloody knife he'd been holding earlier sent a shiver through her. She pushed the vivid images away, unwilling to allow them.

"Would you like to see the rest of my collection?" Thor seemed amused at her discomfort.

She shook her head. Why in the world did he think she wanted to see a bunch of dead animals? She repressed a shudder and looked to Jason for help. The goon that claimed to be her twin had his mouth open, probably planning to say how he wanted to look at lifelike corpses. She glared at him. His eyes crinkled with laughter, but he kept quiet for once.

"So, Mr. Larson, do you have any idea when you'll be available?" Jason gave her a smirk that said she owed him.

"How long will this trip last?" Thor asked.

Jason frowned. "I'm hoping we can finish in two weeks, but it might be best to plan for three just to be on the safe side. Will that be a problem?"

"Usually I only guide for a week at a time." Thor rubbed his chin. Jazmyn could hear the rasp of his beard. Rather than being repulsed by his rough appearance, she felt an almost overwhelming attraction. How could she get out of this trip? She didn't want to spend two or three weeks in close contact with this man. However, Jason would be a problem. Once he got an idea in his head, he clung to it with the tenacity of a bulldog.

For the next hour Jazmyn listened as Jason and Thor finalized plans for the trip. She tried to keep her eyes focused on her hands, but they kept straying as if they had a mind of their own. First she would find herself staring at Thor. Then he would glance over and catch her with that brilliant blue gaze of his. Embarrassed, she would look sideways only to find herself watching the dead dog sleeping in the corner. Finally, she leaned back against the sofa and closed her eyes.

"C'mon, Sis." Jason gave her a swat on the knee, startling her out of her reverie.

"Are we going home now?" Jazmyn regretted the words as soon as they left her mouth. She didn't want them to know she had nearly drifted off, lulled by Thor's deep voice. Since Adam's death she hadn't slept well. At times like this the sleepless nights would catch up with her.

"Not yet." Jason grinned. "We're going with Thor a little further up the mountain. He has a place he thinks I might be interested in photographing. Of course, if you want to wait here, you can sleep with the dog."

Jazmyn bolted off the couch. Her face burned when she looked at Jason's smirk and knew he'd been teasing her. Thor turned his back in an obvious attempt not to laugh. Still, she thought she could detect his shoulders shaking. Wasn't this nice, that he and Jason were such a chummy pair? She should have known. After all, they were like two peas in a pod; both loved adventure and tormenting helpless creatures—like her. Jazmyn stalked regally out the door.

A few minutes later she wished she'd stayed at the cabin to nap with the dead dog. Wedged in the front seat between Jason and Thor with nothing to hold on to, she found herself bouncing into one and then the other. The track they were taking up the mountain made the road to Thor's house look like a four-lane highway.

Potholes deep enough to count as swimming pools checkered the trail. Thor swung from one side to the other like a skier running a slalom course. Trees grew close, towering giants that threatened to tighten their ranks and not let the vehicle through. Pine-needled branches smacked against the side of the truck as if trying to discourage entry to this realm.

Jazmyn tried closing her eyes. A sudden swerve sent her careening against Thor's arm. Her eyes flew open. Thor grinned down at her. For a long moment Jazmyn couldn't look away. She felt as if he could see all the way into her soul.

"Rock." Jason's matter-of-fact statement made her jump.

Thor looked back out the windshield, grunted, and swung sharply to the right, his side-view mirror scraping against a tree. Jazmyn screamed and grabbed Jason's arm. She needed to pray, but her brain refused to function. Between her fear and this irrational attraction, all she could hope for was to be safe once more in her comfortable apartment. As beautiful as these mountains were, she wasn't sure she ever wanted to come back here.

The truck skidded back onto the faint track and straightened out. Jazmyn gripped the cloth so hard her fingers ached.

"If you want to drive, just ask. You don't have to push me out the door." Thor's statement only made her want to wipe the smug look off his face. How could she be so attracted to this man one minute and furious at him the next? It didn't make sense.

She shook the hair from her eyes and tried to scowl. "I didn't realize you called this driving." If he could act like Jason, she could treat him the same.

Thor grinned, swerving around another mudhole, bringing her dangerously close to landing in his lap. Skidding to a stop, he shifted into park before he turned to her. "Your chariot ride is over, my lady. Now the walking begins."

"Walking? You said we would drive to the place." Jazmyn hoped they didn't hear the distress in her voice. Exercise was not high on her priority list. In fact, her idea of a workout was the same as her grandfather's had been—after a bath you drain the water and fight the current.

"We're only going a few hundred yards." Thor looked down at her and shrugged his shoulders. "Of course, you can wait here if you want."

Jazmyn breathed a sigh of relief. "Thanks, I'll stay here if you won't be too long."

"We shouldn't be more than an hour." He rubbed his chin, gazing up into the forest of pines. He opened the door and climbed out to join Jason, who looked like an eager puppy ready to bound off into the woods. Thor leaned casually against the door and studied her with his piercing blue eyes.

"If any bears come by, just ignore them." His deep voice boomed like a death knell. She pictured huge bears lumbering out of the woods in droves. "Be sure to keep the doors locked and you'll be safe. They rarely break out glass." His words sent her scrambling for the door at the same time Thor slammed it shut.

❧

Thor swung the door shut and held his breath, stifling the

laughter in his throat. He could hear his mother saying he should be ashamed of himself, but that look of abject terror in Jazmyn's eyes had been worth the teasing. Besides, for some unexplainable reason he wanted her to stay with them.

He wouldn't admit this to anyone, although he suspected Jason might have guessed the truth—he could have done a lot less swerving around potholes if he'd wanted. Instead, he found himself relishing the contact with Jazmyn. The scent of her lingered, along with the ripples of sensation created by her touch.

"Wait." Jazmyn swung the door open, bolted from the vehicle, and almost ran over them catching up. "I think I will go along." She walked close to Jason, but her eyes were swinging from one tree to the next as if watching for any wild animals that might want to have her for lunch.

The climb uphill wasn't too steep, but Thor knew that for someone unused to exercise it would be a strain. He kept the pace slow, stopping to point out various mosses and small wildlife to give Jazmyn a chance to catch her breath. He knew Jason understood why he kept stopping, but he had a hard time understanding his own motives. Normally, he would take a perverse pleasure in setting a grueling pace just to show city slickers how ill-prepared they were for the mountains. Between the climbing and the thin air, they quickly became short of breath and begged for a break.

With Jazmyn he felt different. For some strange reason he wanted to help her to enjoy the experience. He shook his head and stopped to point out a squirrel scolding them from a branch above. When Jazmyn couldn't find it, he pulled her close, cheek to cheek, directing her until her eyes lit up with pleasure at seeing the squirrel. The closeness brought to life feelings he didn't want to explore. He released her and stepped away, stalking on toward the overlook. He was glad he wouldn't see her again after today. He'd sworn off women, their lies, and all the trouble they brought with them.

The faint rumble of the falls grew louder. The ground vibrated beneath their feet. Thor motioned, and Jason and Jazmyn followed his every move as they approached the cliff overlooking the forest pool. They didn't have to be quiet. The sound of the waterfall covered any noise they made. Wildlife frequently drank from the pool at the base of the falls. Thor hoped they wouldn't startle any deer or elk that happened to be there.

Within minutes he gestured for Jazmyn to sit with him on the rocks at the edge of the cliff. Jason dropped down on her other side. Her face paled a little as she peered over the edge of the steep drop-off. Hunkering down, she eased forward until she rested next to him. Her feet swung over empty space, while her fingers whitened from their grip on the rocks.

Jason and Jazmyn were speechless, staring at the beauty in the glade below. The waterfall plunged over rocks decorated with green moss into a mirror-like pool bordered by a carpet of jade-colored grass. A mixture of pine, scrub oak, and spruce trees circled the edge of the clearing. Various ferns grew on the hillside. A small stream bubbled and churned, wending its way down the mountain.

A doe stepped out from the trees, her long ears flicking back and forth as she stood like a statue checking for danger. At a silent signal she moved forward, and two fawns leaped from the forest to gambol across the grass toward the water. Their spotted backs twitched as they cavorted on their spindly legs.

Jazmyn gripped Thor's arm, apparently oblivious to her actions, and her mouth formed a silent O. She stared as if mesmerized by the scene below. Thor couldn't help studying her face. The climb had brought a rosy hue to her pale complexion. A strand of red-gold hair drifted across her cheek. He longed to brush the stray lock back into place.

As if sensing his perusal she lifted her eyes and looked at him. He had the wild urge to kiss her. For that enchanted look in her green eyes, he, Thor the unapproachable, felt like he would do almost anything.

three

Downshifting, Thor eased his truck into the crossing, the waters coming higher than in most years. The mountains had gotten a lot of rain in the last month, resulting in the rushing river.

"That's okay, boys." He grinned at his dogs' eager faces. They loved coming to the mountains with him. "This will keep any touristy types from invading our camp."

A dirt track led off into the trees. Thor pulled in and stopped the pickup. Rolling down the window and shutting off the engine, he reveled in the silence of the forest.

Loki scrambled across his lap to stick his head out the window. Tongue lolling, the dog appeared to be laughing in sheer delight at being at the camp again. Thor's cabin might be high by desert standards, but this place was another four thousand feet in elevation. He and his dogs always welcomed the change in temperature.

"Let's go." Thor flung the door open and the dogs leaped out. They rushed about, noses to the ground, checking to see who had been there in their absence. Overhead a squirrel scampered to a higher branch, stopping to scold the dogs for invading her territory.

Thor began to drag equipment from the bed of the truck. He and Jason had planned exactly what each would bring so they could set up camp. The more Thor talked with Jason the more he admired him. Jason knew his way around the woods and a camp. These two weeks could be relaxing and fun, a good break from the stress of running the company.

By the time Thor heard the rumble of Jason's SUV lumbering through the crossing, he had his tent erected and the camp's "kitchen" arranged.

"Hey, Thor," Jason called from his open window as he slowed to a stop beside Thor's truck. The dogs leaped in delighted anticipation. "Sorry we're running a little late."

Thor swung around, muttering under his breath. "Sorry *we're* late?" He stared in horror as a slender figure climbed out of the far side of the SUV. Jazmyn. Jazmyn of the enchanting eyes. Jazmyn, who had haunted his thoughts for the past two weeks. Jazmyn, whom he thought he'd never see again and would soon forget.

Jason bounded forward, grinning, hand outstretched. "I managed to convince Jazmyn to come along and help with the photo shoots." He lowered his voice as he glanced over his shoulder at his sister. "She needs to get away and relax a little. She's strung tight enough to snap."

Acting on autopilot, Thor shook hands with Jason, but his gaze riveted on the woman standing beside the SUV. Her wide eyes drew him in as she stared at him. Thor wanted to argue with Jason about having Jazmyn here, but he could see from her pale, drawn look that she needed this. Nothing healed a worn spirit like time spent in the mountains. Fresh air, camp food, and exercise were sure to help her out.

"Jason, Jazmyn." He nodded in her direction. The thin air seemed to be making him light-headed, a problem he didn't often have. At least not when he was standing still, doing nothing. Maybe she would only stay a couple of days and then go back to the city for her job. For his peace of mind Thor hoped so.

"Jaz had all her accounts up-to-date, so she'll be able to stay for the whole two weeks." Jason flashed a smile at his sister, then lowered his voice. "Of course, she's never been camping before, so this could be quite an experience for her." He gestured at Jazmyn. "Come on over here and say hello."

Still wide-eyed, Jazmyn came over and offered Thor her hand. He had a wild urge to bow and kiss her fingers like some love-crazed knight but caught himself in time only to nod as he wrapped her hand in his.

"Accounts?" Thor asked, trying to make sense of what he'd heard. "Jason said you had your accounts up-to-date." Realizing he still held her hand, he let go. "What kind of accounts?"

"I run a small business from my home. Small-business web pages. I set them up and keep them current."

Thoughts of his own company flashed through Thor's mind. No way would she consider T.L. Enterprises to be small. No one would. Besides, he didn't want her to think of him in any other capacity than that of a backwoods hunting guide. Not with what he knew about the greedy nature of women. He didn't think he could take finding out this beauty was as manipulative as the other females who'd been in his life.

"Come on, Jaz. Let's get everything unloaded in case it starts to rain later," Jason called back over his shoulder. "I brought an extra tent so she could have her own."

Jazmyn stared after Jason's retreating back. "What are you talking about? I'm not sleeping in a tent. There are bears in these woods." She marched after Jason, her back rigid. "What do you mean a tent? You didn't mention this. In fact, you implied we would have access to a motor home. Remember?"

Jason's chuckle sounded forced as he tossed a sleeping bag at his sister. "I had to do something to get you to come. Besides, I never said we would use an RV. I only said that some people use them up here."

Clinging to the sleeping bag, Jazmyn stared, her mouth open. Thor leaned back against his truck and watched. He wasn't about to get in the middle of this.

"What about the bears?" she squeaked.

"Keep food out of your tent, and they won't bother you." The bag of tent poles clanked as Jason tossed them to the ground.

"What if they think I'm food?"

"With your sour disposition?" Jason laughed. "It'll never happen." He threw a second sleeping bag to Jazmyn, then picked up the tent and poles and went to pick out a spot to set up. The dogs lost interest and flopped down under a tree to watch. Thor didn't know whether to offer his help or stay out of the danger zone.

After he covered the kitchen area with a tarp to protect against rain, Thor pulled up a chair, settling in to watch Jason and Jazmyn. He could use a little break, anyway. At first he found them funny. Jason, knowledgeable about camping, barked orders, expecting Jazmyn to follow his rapid-fire instructions. The perpetual look of confusion on her face touched his heart, though. When he noticed the sheen of tears in her eyes, Thor had had enough.

"Why don't you take a break while I help Jason finish this?" he offered, taking the tent pole out of Jazmyn's hands and directing her to the vacated chair. "We'll have this up in no time." He squeezed her shoulder. "You'll be as safe as if you were home in your apartment, maybe safer. Some of the human animals in the city are much more dangerous than the animals in the wild."

Jazmyn blinked and turned away as if trying to hide the fact that she was about to cry. Thor fought the desire to put his arms around her. He'd never had such a strong attraction to a woman before, not even his ex-fiancées.

"It's okay. I came to help out, not to be a burden." Jazmyn's voice quavered.

The list of chores that needed to be done ran through

Thor's mind. He wanted to come up with some job that would make her feel useful, not incompetent.

"On the way up here I stopped and cut enough wood for tonight and tomorrow morning. Why don't I help you up into the back of the truck? You can toss the logs out. Then if you still want something to do, you can stack them between those two trees over there." He pointed at a pair of trees near the fire pit he'd already dug, but not close enough to be a hazard.

❧

After only ten minutes Jazmyn's arm muscles burned. Half the truck bed was piled with logs that Thor seemed to think were nothing more than sticks. She thought some of them weighed more than she did.

She hefted another one, preparing to toss it onto the growing pile beside the pickup. But when she heaved, the log slipped and crashed to the floor of the truck bed, coming to rest on her toe. She shrieked.

"Jaz, you okay?" Jason peered over the side of the truck.

Thor vaulted over the side, his blue eyes full of concern. "What happened?"

"That tree trunk landed on my toe," Jazmyn managed to say as waves of agony shot up her leg.

"Let's get this shoe off and see if the toe's broken." Thor shifted the log until it stood on end. "Here, have a seat." He patted the piece of wood. As soon as she was seated he unlaced her sneaker.

"You should have boots for up here in the mountains." Although he spoke to her, Jazmyn had the distinct impression that Thor's words were directed at Jason.

"Jason told me to bring boots, and I did bring them. I just didn't put them on yet." She gasped as he eased the shoe off. "I thought they were only for hiking."

She closed her eyes as Thor slipped her sock off. The sharp

pain had passed, replaced by throbbing. She didn't want to look, but the sensation of Thor's touch seemed even more dangerous than having a broken toe.

"No blood, Sis. You'll live." Jason sounded like he was holding back laughter. She opened her eyes and glared at him.

"Ouch!" She tried to jerk back from Thor's probing, but he had a firm grip on her foot.

"This might be sore for a few days." He smiled up at her, still holding her foot in his hands. Her pulse raced. Jazmyn tried to convince herself it was from the excitement of the moment and had nothing to do with Thor's touch, or the way she felt as he gazed at her.

"It doesn't look broken. I don't even think you'll lose the nail." Shaking out her sock, he eased it back over her toes carefully.

The image of Thor holding the bloody knife flashed through Jazmyn's mind again as it had a hundred times since the day she met him. In the past two weeks she'd convinced herself the man was a danger to society. She'd been terrified of coming up here with Jason but even more terrified to have Jason come alone. This man, treating her with such compassion, wasn't the same man who'd invaded her thoughts for the past few weeks. How could she ever have thought he would harm them?

"There you go." Thor held out a hand to help her to her feet. "I'd better get back to helping Jason. We still have a lot to do." He tossed the offending log from the truck as if it weighed nothing, then vaulted to the ground. Turning, he held out his hand. As she slipped over the side and landed on the ground, Jazmyn did her best not to wince. For some reason she wanted to show Thor she could be a good camper. She wanted him to like her.

four

Staring into the crackling flames, Jazmyn didn't think life could get much worse. Every muscle in her body ached. Her toe throbbed. She'd been humiliated beyond what she ever thought possible. This may well have been the worst day of her life.

Jesus, You promised to come back for Your people. Now might be a real good time. She raised a questioning eyebrow at the night sky. Visions of being whisked up to heaven made her sigh. No more pain. No more humiliation. "How soon can I get there?" She glanced over her shoulder hoping no one had heard her. That's all she needed, for Thor to believe she was loony enough to talk to herself.

Jason and Thor were nowhere in sight. She didn't know what mischief they were up to now. All afternoon Jason had tormented her with one thing or another. To his credit, Thor hadn't actually done anything to her, but she'd seen him trying to hide a smile once or twice.

For years she hadn't been interested in men. Her mother had convinced her they all were bad. Then she met Adam and that opinion dissolved. When Adam died, Jazmyn wanted everything else to end, too. For the first time in two years, she'd met a man she might be interested in, and all she could do was make a fool of herself.

She sighed. This wasn't meant to be, anyway. Thor might make her react to him physically, but she had the feeling he wasn't on the same wavelength spiritually. She and Jason had had several longs talks about being unequally yoked, as the Bible called it. They had even attended a singles class at church on the perils of dating someone who didn't share your faith. She'd determined not to fall into that trap if she ever decided to date again.

Then why do I have to be attracted to a man who isn't a Christian? The question had plagued her for most of the afternoon.

The lantern Thor hung from a tree hissed into the night. Moths and other small insects hovered around the bright light, swooping and dipping in a graceful waltz.

The low rumble of male laughter drifted to her. She supposed Jason and Thor were still doing something to finish the camp setup. They'd both been fanatical about seeing that everything was in its place.

She'd felt nothing but helpless all afternoon. Every time she tried to step in and do something, they took over because she was doing it wrong. Even the way she stacked the wood was wrong, so Jason redid the whole pile. She wanted to scream.

Closing her eyes, she listened to the ripple of the river rushing past their camp. No cars. No sirens. No helicopters or planes. Absolute quiet could be unnerving. She almost wanted to jump up and yell, "Where is everybody?" How could anyone find this peaceful? Even Thor and Jason were quiet now.

From the corner of her eye she caught movement. Expecting her brother to be sneaking up on her, she stared into the fire. He wouldn't pull a fast one on her this time. She was prepared.

A slight dragging noise came from that side of the camp. Jason was being quiet, but she knew exactly where he was. She would wait till he was right behind her, then jump up and scare him. She grinned. That would serve him right, especially if Thor were there to witness her triumph instead of another defeat.

Her heart pounded. Sweat dampened her palms. A snuffling noise and another slight motion came from closer to her chair. She tensed, ready to leap to her feet.

Another burst of laughter rang out from across the camp. Jazmyn frowned. How could Jason be over there laughing and also sneaking up on her? What were they up to, anyway?

Something dark drifted into the ring of lantern light. Heart thudding, Jazmyn felt like the heroine in a horror movie, forwarding in slow motion, as she turned her head to look. A skunk, the size of a small dog, ambled toward her and the fire. The movement she'd spotted from the corner of her eye had to be the gentle motion of the black and white tail rising up and down. Her stomach knotted.

"Jason." Her constricted throat released the word as a squeaky whisper. The skunk paused a moment before continuing toward her.

Jazmyn wanted to leap off the chair and run for safety. How far did a skunk spray? Didn't a raised tail mean the beast was getting ready to douse everything with foul-smelling scent? She froze as the animal wandered nearer, too terrified even to draw her legs up onto the chair.

Two smaller versions of the approaching pest trotted into the light. Jazmyn sank tighter against the back of her seat, praying the fabric wouldn't tear and spill her to the ground. One of the babies scampered up on the rocks of the fire pit and began to sniff.

Earlier, after he'd gotten the fire going, Jason had burned all the trash from their meal. The baby skunk must have smelled the lingering aroma. Jazmyn clenched her fists as the small skunk leaned over and pawed at the coals. What would the mother skunk do if the baby caught on fire?

"Shoo." The baby didn't even look up. "Go away." Jazmyn knew these wild animals would never heed her quiet whisper, but that was all she could manage at the moment. She didn't know how this situation could get much worse.

Something brushed against Jazmyn's pant leg. She stared in horror as the mother skunk wound her way through her legs, the long fur of the skunk's tail waving in the slight breeze. If this were happening on television, Jazmyn might be able to appreciate how cute these animals were. As it was, only her terror glued her to her seat.

"Jaz, don't move," Jason said from somewhere behind her. She wanted to ask if he thought she was stupid. Was she going to jump up and down or something?

"We're going to make some noise. They'll leave the camp." Thor stepped into the shadows off to her left. She could see from the corner of her eye that he held a bucket and a stick.

"What are you doing?" She was already preparing for the onslaught of skunk scent.

"They don't like this sound. Don't jump. Stay still." Thor lifted the stick and beat on the bucket like a drummer from some band.

The baby skunk jumped down from the rocks. The mother scampered off toward the shadows, her babies close behind. Jazmyn's muscles cramped from being tensed so long.

"Relax, Sis." Jason's heavy pat to her back reverberated through her. "You probably would have lost the scent by the time we got back to civilization." His laughter chased after the skunks.

❧

"Once we get the camp set up, we'll start looking for the wildlife you want to shoot." Thor picked up the axe, hefting it to get the feel just right before he started splitting wood. Jason was finishing the tarps over the kitchen area. With the building clouds, having the tarps up was important.

"What will we be looking at first?" Jason asked.

Thor caught a glimpse of Jazmyn stepping from rock to rock down by the river. Ever since the episode with the skunks last night, she'd changed. Before she'd been uncertain about the mountains and the wildlife here. Now she appeared afraid of everything. Her gaze roved the hills around them, and she avoided areas of dense brush or high grass. Every new sound made her jump. The dark circles under her eyes told Thor she hadn't slept well last night.

"I thought we might try to find some elk. I've seen a large herd not far from here." Thor gestured toward Jazmyn with his chin. "Has she ever been in the mountains before?"

Jason shook his head. "Naw. She doesn't get out much. Stays shut up in her apartment and works on her computer. She's had some emotional setbacks. This trip may be hard, but I think it will be good for her."

"I'm thinking for her first time camping, the experience might have been better in a more controlled setting."

Jason shrugged. "You could be right. She's tough, though. I wanted something to shock her out of the depression she's been in."

"If you wanted shock, this should do it." Thor set up a log, stepped back, and prepared to swing the axe. Jason moved away to finish the tarps.

The pile of split logs grew as Thor swung the axe. After the first ten minutes, he removed his long-sleeved shirt. The cool air dried the sweat that had built up in the short time he'd been working. This was one of his favorite jobs in camp. Something about the rhythmic swing of the axe and the bite into the wood satisfied him.

From the corner of his eye he kept a watch on Jazmyn. The lack of sparkle in her eyes bothered him. He wanted to do something to help her adjust to the mountains. By the time he finished the splitting and stacking, he had an idea of what to do.

Curled up in a chair reading a book, Jazmyn looked pale and vulnerable when he approached her later. She glanced up, her luminous green eyes a little dull, from fatigue he guessed. Thor smiled.

"Jason says you haven't done much camping before."

She chewed her lower lip, an action he found fascinating. "This will probably be my only camping trip. I don't plan to let him trick me into doing it again." Moisture glistened in her eyes.

"I thought you might like to help out with the cooking." Thor hunkered down so he wouldn't appear to tower over her. "It's different from cooking at home, but the food always seems to taste better. I don't know if it's the air or just being outdoors, but eating in the mountains is a different experience."

"I can't imagine this being better than picking up a sandwich or soup at the corner deli."

"Then you haven't done enough work around camp." Thor grinned. "Are you game enough to help out?"

She nodded. He stood and held out his hand to help her from the chair. As he drew her up, he noticed a slight flush stain her cheeks. He wondered what thoughts were making her blush. Did she feel an attraction to him? Memories of another woman who acted coy and blushed, then broke his heart, sent a shaft of anger coursing through him. He let go of Jazmyn's hand and swung around to stalk off toward the kitchen area.

"I'm finished with the tarps. I'll get some water," Jason called as he set off toward the river swinging two buckets at his side. A breeze ruffled his hair.

"I want to show you how to work the stove first," Thor said as Jazmyn caught up to him. He unscrewed the pump on the gas tank. "Before you use one of these stoves, you have to pump the tank to build up pressure. Sometimes you have to pump a little during the cooking to keep the right pressure."

He demonstrated by pulling the knob out and plunging it back in. Holding the stove tight with one hand, Thor kept up the pumping action for a few seconds.

"Here, you try it." He stepped back to make room for Jazmyn. Her first try had the pump plunging in fast, but without doing any good. She looked at Thor in frustration.

"Here." He put his fingers over hers. "You need to cover this hole in order for the pressure to build." He tightened his hand and helped her to pump the stove.

"How do you know when you've done enough?"

Thor let go and Jazmyn continued to work the lever. "It depends on how full the tank is. Since I just filled it, you won't need to pump as long. You'll feel the pressure building and it will get harder to do."

She caught her lower lip between her teeth, concentration furrowing her brow. Thor admired her willingness to try this. Most of the women he'd known wouldn't go to the mountains unless it was winter and they were housed at a lodge for skiing.

"That's good." Thor showed her how to screw the pump shut. "Now you turn this lever up, light your match, and open the line for the gas to come out." He scraped a match along the stove and touched it to the burner. Flames shot up several inches. Jazmyn gasped and jumped back. Thor chuckled. "Don't worry. That's the way this stove lights."

He began to pump the lever again. "The flame will calm down in a minute. When that happens you turn this lever down, adjust the flame to the right heat, and you're ready to cook."

Thor plunked an iron skillet filled with hamburger meat on the grill over the burner. "We can make some sloppy joes for lunch. How are you at chopping onion?" He cocked an eyebrow, trying to ignore how much he enjoyed having Jazmyn here beside him. The picture of her helping him out around the camp was almost too appealing. Maybe encouraging her to cook wasn't the best idea.

"I'll have you know I'm an expert at chopping onions," she said. Thor gazed down into Jazmyn's eyes. A slight smile lit her features.

"Hey, Thor, we have company," Jason called out from near the river.

Jazmyn's eyes grew wide with horror as she stared past Thor. All color drained from her face. Thor swung around to see a black bear ambling down the hill toward them.

five

"That's the last of it." Jason backed out of the truck after stowing his photography equipment behind the seat.

A hush lay over the forest. Thor glanced again at Jazmyn's tent, wanting to know if she was okay, but knowing it wasn't his place to approach her until she came out. Jason had already given her a wake-up call. Last night Jason had spent quite awhile with Jazmyn, talking to her and reading to her from the Bible. Thor hadn't interfered. He only hoped what Jason said helped Jazmyn sleep. After the incident with the bear, she'd been too terrified to do much.

Bears sometimes wandered into camp in the mountains. If they were hungry and smelled food, they came to investigate. In a regular camping area, the forest service did their best to keep the sites free of bears, but out here nature took over. Fortunately, the bear hadn't stuck around. When Thor waved his arms and yelled, the creature changed its mind about being hungry. These small blacks weren't very aggressive.

But Jazmyn, having never camped in the mountains before, didn't understand this. She associated bears with attacks and mutilation. She'd been in a state of abject terror for most of the afternoon.

The sound of a zipper swung Thor's attention back to her tent. She stepped out, one hand still on the flap, as if she would jump back in if need be. Her nose wrinkled. Thor breathed deep, noting the pine scent of the forest and knowing that's what she was smelling, too. He wondered if she enjoyed breathing in this fresh air as much as he did.

"Good morning." He smiled at her.

"Morning? More like the middle of the night, you mean." At least she retained her sense of humor.

"C'mon, Sis, you're slowing us down," Jason said. "Let's go."

"Without breakfast? No coffee?" Jazmyn's eyes widened. Thor recalled that she hadn't eaten enough to keep a bug alive yesterday. She had to be hungry this morning.

"I've already poured you a cup of coffee." Jason held up a travel cup. "Grab a granola bar and hop in. Your chariot awaits." He gave a courtly bow, one hand motioning toward the truck.

For the first time Thor noticed Jazmyn's attire. She wore jeans, hiking boots, and a T-shirt. Her jacket must still be inside. She stood there rubbing her arms, shivering.

"Where's your jacket?" he asked.

Her teeth chattered. "Do you realize where I come from the temperature is over a hundred degrees in the daytime? The nights aren't cold, either." She shrugged. "I wore my only long-sleeved shirt yesterday."

"You didn't bring a jacket?" Thor wanted to throttle Jason. Hadn't he realized Jazmyn wouldn't know what kind of clothes to bring to the mountains if she'd never been here before?

"Hey, I told her to bring something warm," Jason said.

"You told me sometimes it gets cool in the mountains. I brought the only flannel shirt I owned for the nights. I didn't expect the mornings to be so cold." She blinked several times.

Jason shook his head and ran a hand through his hair. "Sorry, Jaz. I didn't think about you not knowing what to bring. I've been going to the mountains so many years I just assumed everyone knew how to pack."

Thor reached Jazmyn in three strides. Her eyes grew round as she watched him stalking toward her. Tugging off his jacket, he wrapped it around her shoulders. He wanted to draw her into his arms and hold her until she stopped shivering, but he resisted the urge.

"I can't take your coat. You'll be cold."

He let his hands linger a moment on her shoulders. "I don't get too cold up here. I'm used to the cooler temperatures. Besides, I have a spare jacket in the truck. Ready to go?"

She nodded, shrugging into the jacket. She looked like a little girl playing dress-up in clothes several sizes too big. She was so adorable. He slipped his hand under her elbow and led her to the truck. Jason joined them with steaming cups of coffee, several granola bars protruding from his pockets.

"Why do we have to get up so early?" Jazmyn stifled a yawn as Thor fired up the truck. "Aren't the animals still sleeping?"

Jason laughed. "This is prime time for animal viewing. Early morning and dusk are the best times to find the elk and deer out feeding. The best light will be about the time we get there. Just because you sleep till noon doesn't mean the rest of the world does."

Jazmyn's cheeks pinkened. She lifted the coffee to her lips and took a tentative sip. Thor thought about telling Jason he had to treat his sister better or walk to the herd of elk. He blew out a breath. He liked Jason. For the most part he was a decent sort, but when it came to Jazmyn, he constantly baited her.

"What kind of animals are we going to see first?" she asked.

Before Thor could answer, Jason piped up. "We're going for the bears first." He peeled the wrapper from a granola bar. "I missed filming the one in camp yesterday afternoon, so we're going to find a few today."

Clenching his jaw, Thor fought back anger. Why did Jason do this to Jazmyn? "If you want to see bear, you'll have to hop out and hoof it. I'm taking you to the herd of elk like we planned earlier."

"Well, I guess I'll have to settle for them, then." Jason grinned and held out a packet to Jazmyn. "Granola bar?"

She took the proffered bar. Thor noted how she'd moved a little closer to him. He wanted to put his arm around her and tell her he wouldn't let anything bad happen, but he couldn't do that. Besides, he needed both hands to drive as he swung off the main road onto the track leading into the forest.

"Do all these places have to be so rough?" Jazmyn lifted her coffee cup, trying to keep the hot liquid from spilling as they thumped through a pothole.

"You don't find herds of wildlife along the interstate," Jason quipped. "They're out here because people don't come here often. They don't enjoy the malls or shopping."

"Once you get used to these roads, they aren't so bad," Thor said, ignoring Jason's comment. "Think of it in terms of people who refuse to use a computer because they don't understand them. Once they start using one they begin to enjoy what they can do."

"I'm not sure I see the comparison between computers and the middle-of-nowhere." Jazmyn's eyes twinkled.

Thor chuckled. "I'm just trying to say that a lot of people are afraid of the unknown, but when they get used to something, it can become enjoyable."

Jazmyn fell against him as he swung to miss a deep rut. "I can't imagine ever finding this enjoyable," she said. Thor looked away, not wanting her to read the disappointment in his eyes.

◆

The engine strained as they crawled up a ridge. Jazmyn felt sure mountain goats would have trouble bounding up this track.

She tried to focus on the trees outside Thor's window so she wouldn't see the drop-off on Jason's side. If she looked out the windshield, the steep rise in front of them made her dizzy, too. Thor glanced down at her, his azure gaze making her as dizzy as the drop-off. She closed her eyes, certain there wasn't a safe place to look.

"Here we are." Thor's deep voice brought her out of her reverie.

Opening her eyes, Jazmyn gasped. Through the forest she could see a small open meadow ringed with trees. Bars of sunlight filtered between the branches, giving the scene a surreal quality. On the far side of the clearing, a few long-legged shapes moved through the remnants of the mist.

"This is spectacular." Jason's hushed whisper startled Jazmyn. "I need to get my equipment out and set up before the fog burns off." He eased the door open and clambered out.

Thor placed a hand on Jazmyn's arm as she started to follow Jason. She turned to find him staring down at her.

"I know you're not familiar with the wildlife here. These elk are as shy as any animal can be. We have to move quietly. No talking, either. If they see that we're here, they'll be gone just like that." He snapped his fingers and winked at her. Jazmyn thought she might agree to anything he said at that moment.

Outside the truck she pulled the jacket close against the chill air, savoring the man-scent on the coat. Thor strode around the front of the truck. "Need any help, Jason?"

"No." Jason dug through a bag, retrieving various lenses and film. "I'm not setting up a tripod or anything." He glanced at Jazmyn and then back at Thor. "If you want to help, you can make sure Jazmyn doesn't meet up with anything wild that makes her scream."

Jazmyn glared at him.

"I'm serious, Jaz. If you make any noise and scare these animals off, I'll feed you to the bears myself." He grinned to soften his words.

They watched as he slipped through the trees to the edge of the clearing. Jazmyn didn't know whether to be angry with her brother or not. He'd wanted her to come along, supposedly to help out. Now he didn't seem to want her here at all.

"Why don't we take a walk along the ridge?" Thor's hand grasped her elbow. Jazmyn couldn't remember when he'd taken her arm, but she enjoyed his touch. Wonder filled her at that knowledge. She hadn't wanted a man to touch her since Adam, or before Adam, either. What was it about Thor that was so different she found herself attracted to him?

"Will we scare off the elk?" she whispered.

"Not if we're careful." Thor began to walk, guiding her to a narrow trail. "We might even find a good vantage point where we can watch without endangering the filming."

Jazmyn almost laughed. "This sounds like a movie. Do you suppose the elk ladies are all made up and ready for their big day?"

Thor grinned. Her heart skipped a beat. "These ladies wear their finery every day."

As they continued along the ridge the sun burned off all the fog. This would be a bright beautiful morning. Thor had mentioned they should have rain by the afternoon, but right now there wasn't a cloud in the sky.

Staying away from the cliff edge kept Jazmyn's mind off Thor. She'd never thought she would be attracted to someone rough and rugged. Adam had been into computers. They had so much in common. They would talk for hours about their businesses, customers, and ways they would combine their enterprises once they were married. What would she and Thor ever have to talk about? Past pets? The various ways to chop an onion?

A high cry pierced the air. Jazmyn froze. Thor stepped up beside her. "Look." He pointed up at the sky. A gray-white bird soared overhead, graceful and free.

"What is it?" Jazmyn stared in awe at the beautiful sight.

"It's an osprey." Thor wasn't watching the bird anymore. He seemed to be looking up at the trees instead.

"Look, there." He pointed again, this time at a clump of pine trees. Jazmyn tried to figure out what he wanted her to see.

"See the dead tree, right in the middle?" Thor leaned close, helping her to sight on the right one. "Near the top of that tree."

She stared in the direction he indicated, found the pine, and let her gaze travel to the top. She drew in a sharp breath. "It's a nest."

"That's where the osprey has its young. Watch." The bird circled a few more times then glided down toward its babies.

"What's it carrying?"

"Breakfast," Thor said, smiling. "She's been out fishing and is carrying her catch back for the babies."

"Breakfast in bed? I don't think I would want stinky fish crumbs in there with me."

His low, throaty laugh warmed her. She couldn't help but join him.

"We'd better keep going if we want to see the elk." This time he led her off the path into the trees. "I think we've come far enough, but we'll have to be quiet from here on out."

They wound through the tall pines with Thor doing his best to keep them from making much noise. He often pointed out sticks to her, keeping her from stepping on them and making a loud snap.

As they approached the meadow Thor slowed. From behind him Jazmyn couldn't see much. She didn't want to look around him for fear of making too much commotion. She had no doubt Jason would feed her to the bears, or do some other horrible thing, if she ruined this opportunity.

Thor stopped. He motioned her to come up beside him. Jewel-green grass dotted with yellow flowers sparkled in the clearing. All the morning mist had departed, but dew clung in a heavy coat. They both crouched down, gazing in awe at the graceful elk.

Jazmyn didn't know how long they watched the herd or how long Thor had been holding her hand. The moment seemed magical. He pointed across the meadow. She could see Jason crouched at the edge shooting pictures.

Something thudded on her head and bounced off onto the ground. She looked at Thor from the corner of her eye. Had he done something to her? She looked around. There weren't any other animals around, and the elk hadn't thrown anything.

Thump. A second time something hit her head.

She tugged Thor's sleeve. "Did you—?"

He shushed her with a finger to his lips. Three of the elk closest to them swung their heads up, grass still sticking out from their mouths. They took a couple of nervous steps, then seemed to sense there wasn't any trouble and went back to eating.

Scrabbling sounded overhead. Jazmyn looked up just in time to see a brown blur before something hit her in the middle of her forehead.

six

"Ouch!" Jazmyn slapped her hand to her forehead. Her skin stung as if she'd been pricked by a hundred needles.

Thunder rumbled, although there wasn't a cloud in the sky. It took her a moment to realize the sound was that of the elk racing across the field. She'd done what Jason said not to do—make the herd stampede before he'd finished his pictures.

"I'm dead." Dread filled her even as she pulled her fingers away, noting a trace of red on them.

"What happened?" Thor asked.

"Something hit me." She pointed at her forehead, hoping there was at least some sign that she'd been wounded.

He pulled a handkerchief from his pocket and dabbed at her forehead. "What in the world hit you?"

"I don't know. I was just sitting here watching the elk and something hit my head twice." She hesitated, giving him a sheepish smile. "I thought you might be playing a joke on me. Then I looked up and, wham, this thing smacked into me."

A few drops of blood stained his handkerchief. He frowned and stared up into the trees. "There's your attacker." He pointed at an upper branch. A squirrel skittered along, hurrying to get to the trunk of the tree. "She must have been eating the seeds out of the pine cones and throwing the cones down when she finished. You happened to be right under her. These squirrels can get territorial, but they don't normally attack people."

He grinned. "We'd better get back and see how Jason fared. I'm hoping the elk didn't run over the top of him."

Jason wasn't as angry as she thought he'd be. In fact, he was excited. "You won't believe the pictures I got! I'd taken two rolls of film of the elk grazing and the calves playing. Then, when I was almost ready to quit, thinking I wouldn't get any other good pictures, they all started to run toward me. I can't wait to get that film developed." His voice rose as his hands acted out what happened. "I've never been that close or had an opportunity like that."

Thor's eyes twinkled with their secret as Jason wondered aloud what had spooked the herd. Jazmyn wasn't going to tell him. She didn't think Thor would, either.

By the time they returned to camp, it was almost noon. Jazmyn was starving. "If that bear comes back today, he won't stand a chance. I'll eat him," she grumbled as she slid out of the cab of the truck. The granola bar had worn off long ago. Her whole body felt battered and sore. She couldn't remember the last time she'd walked so much. To top it off, all this walking was either uphill or downhill. By tomorrow morning she wouldn't be able to move.

After a quick lunch of sandwiches and chips, Jazmyn relaxed in a chair with her Bible. She hadn't done her study that morning because they left before it was light enough to read. Last night Jason had talked to her about her fears and how she needed to trust God more. He said she wasn't allowing God to lead in her life when everything made her afraid. Being a new Christian, she wasn't sure what to think, but she wanted to take the time to study some of the Scriptures he'd written down for her.

She'd only copied two Scriptures in her notebook when Thor pulled a chair close and sat down. "I thought you and Jason read the Bible last night. Wasn't that enough for the week?"

She started to laugh, then realized he was serious. "I like to study every day. In fact, I have to."

"Why is that? Does your church have some sort of rule about it?"

She smiled. "No. There's so much to learn. Every time I read the Bible I find something new that I didn't know before." Jazmyn paused, trying to decide how to explain the Bible's importance. "You know how new things come with instruction manuals so you can learn how to work them?" She waited for Thor to nod. "Well, the Bible is like an instruction manual for me. It's God's way of telling me how to live my life. In order to know, though, I have to take the time to read and study the manual."

Thor shifted. "I'm not much on reading manuals. I like to figure things out for myself."

Jazmyn didn't know what to say. She wished Jason were here to join the conversation. He always seemed to know the right thing to say about his beliefs. She was so new she didn't even know for sure what she believed. How could she ever convince a doubter like Thor?

"Hey, there are our friends." He gestured behind her.

She stiffened. "The skunks?"

He laughed. "No, they won't be out until after dark. These guys aren't nearly as stinky. Take a look."

First skunks, then bears. Now what was invading their camp? Swiveling in her chair, Jazmyn watched two chipmunks chase each other across the open area near the table. Their tiny tails shot straight up in the air like little masts.

The first one stopped. The second jumped on the first one. They rolled around, and then the chase began again. Jazmyn couldn't help laughing. She'd never seen anything so cute.

"I don't remember seeing them yesterday." She watched as one chipmunk raced into the trees while the other decided to explore the camp.

"They're sometimes a little shy the first day you're here.

Then they come out to scavenge. The squirrels will be out, too. You have to be careful what you leave around, because they can get into almost anything."

"Do you ever leave food out for them?" Jazmyn gasped as the small chipmunk disappeared up the truck tire. "We have to get him out of there." She started to get up. Thor placed his hand on her shoulder, and she sank back.

"He's just being nosy. He won't stay there long." As if to prove Thor's point, the striped animal leaped back to the ground.

"As far as feeding them, I sometimes leave out little scraps in the morning. I don't want to entice bears into the camp. In the mornings the squirrels, chipmunks, and blue jays will fight over anything you leave out for them. They're very fond of pancakes."

"Then if you ever allow me to have breakfast, I want pancakes so I can feed them."

Thor chuckled. "I'll get up early tomorrow and make pancakes before we leave. Then, if you want to stay in camp, you can share your breakfast."

"Stay in camp by myself?"

"There's nothing to be afraid of. The bear won't come back. If it does, you only have to yell and wave your arms to scare it away. There aren't any grizzly bears around here. Most of the black bears are easily frightened off."

Like me. Jazmyn couldn't help the thought. Here she'd been studying the Scriptures Jason gave her about fear, and within a few minutes she'd forgotten them all. How could she ever grow as a Christian at this rate?

ఇ

For the next two days Thor tried his best to ignore Jazmyn, but it proved impossible. From a fearful, timid city girl, she was changing to become accustomed to outdoor life faster than he would have dreamed possible. He watched her patiently coax the tiny chipmunks closer until one took a piece of bread from her hand.

When that happened her gaze met his, and a jolt of pure attraction seared through him. By the time he turned away he felt as if a smile were permanently etched on his face. He grabbed up the axe, splitting more wood in the hopes of taking his mind off the strawberry blonde in his camp.

Every day they were up before sunrise. Jazmyn refused to wait in camp, insisting she be allowed to accompany them on the photo sessions. Jason still baited her, but now Thor knew the reason for her brother's constant teasing.

When he'd pressured Jason about his treatment of Jazmyn, Jason had been hesitant to reply at first.

"You have to understand the situation Jazmyn grew up in." Jason stared at Thor for a long moment as if judging how much he could be trusted. "Our mother had emotional problems. When she and Dad divorced, the courts allowed her to take Jazmyn, while I stayed with Dad. Dad tried to visit and take Jazmyn places, but Mom blocked him at every turn."

"She didn't abuse her, did she?" Thor knew how hard divorce could be, but he couldn't imagine what Jason was leading up to.

"No, not in the physical sense." Jason frowned. "Mom was afraid of people. Later they discovered she had schizophrenia. She would be normal one minute and terrified of everyone the next. She kept Jazmyn cooped up in the house and taught her to fear everything."

He shook his head. "For years Dad and I lost track of them. Mom would move and not tell us where she'd gone. Dad was afraid of going through the courts. He worried about what would happen to Mom. Then later he felt that he'd failed Jazmyn. It was a terrible position to be in."

"I can see that." Thor could almost feel the man's hurt. What a tough decision to make.

"When I made contact with Jazmyn again, she was scared of her own shadow." Jason's lips thinned. "I found the only way to draw her out was to make her angry or make her laugh. I've been spending my time doing one or the other since then. She's come a long way."

The snippet of conversation faded. Thor found himself once again watching Jazmyn as she pursed her lips and made little kissing noises at the chipmunk. If he didn't get ahold of his feelings, she'd have him eating out of her hand by the end of this trip. He swung the axe over his head and buried it in the chunk of aspen. The two log halves flew in either direction from the force of the blow.

He chopped and restacked wood for the next hour, building up a sweat. The sight of Jazmyn, her hand outstretched, a smile lighting her face, refused to leave his mind no matter how hard he tried. If he kept this up, all their decent-sized logs would be kindling.

"What are we fixing for supper tonight?" Thor turned to find Jazmyn at his elbow. Her red-gold hair swung in a pony-tail except for one wavy strand that had escaped and wove a sinuous pattern down her cheek.

Glancing up at the tilt of the sun in the sky, he fought to get his emotions under control. His chest felt as if a band of iron were tightening around him. He had to get out of here and away from this woman. He didn't know how, but she must have found out his secret and was using her wiles to trap him. Tomorrow he would escape.

"I'll throw some oak wood on the fire and cook pork chops." Thor leaned the axe against the tree trunk. "You can get some potatoes ready to bake in the coals. I'll show you where the potatoes and foil are."

He stalked away, doing his best to ignore the hurt in her eyes. The gruffness of his tone had startled even him. *That's okay. Maybe if she thinks I'm the ogre she first believed me to be, she won't turn on the charm so much.*

By the time Thor got the fire ready to cook, Jazmyn had the potatoes wrapped. Jason returned from his late-afternoon walk along the river for pictures. They ate in a companionable silence, each lost in his or her own thoughts.

Jason pushed back his plate and sighed. "It was nice to have a safe meal for a change." He flashed Jazmyn a grin. "I figured Jazmyn couldn't do much to food cooked over the coals."

"I'll have you know I fixed the potatoes." She lifted her nose as if putting on airs.

"Yeah, but there isn't much you can do to them." Jason chuckled. "They weren't burnt, because Thor watched over them."

Jazmyn leaned forward. Her eyes narrowed. "I marked which one was yours. Didn't you notice the small tear-and-repair job done to your foil?" She motioned to the wadded up wrapper from his potato.

"So what kind of poison did you use, Sis?" Jason lowered his voice as if he were in on some conspiracy.

"It wasn't poison." Jazmyn folded her arms over her chest. "You're my brother. I wouldn't do that." An impish look crossed her face. "You remember that plant Thor showed us yesterday? Poison ivy? You swore you could even eat it and you wouldn't have an allergic reaction. I rubbed that on your potato. We'll see if you were right."

Thor tipped his head back and roared. Jason gaped in astonishment.

"I think you've been had this time, Jason. She's getting better." Thor slapped Jason on the shoulder. "That must mean it's your turn for doing dishes."

Jason groaned. "Can't we just leave them out and let the bears lick them clean? That works for me."

"I don't think so." Jazmyn glared at her brother, her hands on her hips. "We're not leaving out any bear bait unless you're attached to it."

seven

The sky was still dark when Thor rolled out of his sleeping bag. Shivering in the predawn chill, he jerked on his clothes. His eyes felt gritty. Sleep had eluded him last night. Instead of the murmur of the river lulling him to sleep, visions of Jazmyn laughing, pensive, fearful filled his mind.

Stepping outside, he took a deep breath of the fresh mountain air. He'd always loved coming here for the solitude and peace, but this trip that contentment had been absent. He couldn't relax. His whole being seemed to be attuned to Jazmyn's presence. He didn't like that.

Faint grayness in the sky, seen through the tall pines, showed that dawn wasn't far off. Thor went about gathering what he needed, waiting for Jason to get up. Jason would try to talk him out of this, of course, but Thor was determined to carry through with what he had to do. He snapped his fingers. Loki and Odin leaped into the bed of the truck. They lay down waiting for him to lead them on a new adventure.

As he loaded the last of what he wanted to take into his pickup, Thor heard the hiss of a zipper. Jason stepped outside, closed his tent, then stood and stretched. His hair stuck up at all angles. He and Jazmyn bore a strong resemblance to one another. Thor wondered, even if Jazmyn hadn't come with Jason, if he still would have been reminded of her every day. After all, how many times had his thoughts strayed to her since that first meeting?

"Mornin'." Jason drew in a deep breath. He, too, appreciated the outdoors. Thor liked that about Jason. In fact, he

51

liked a lot about Jason, although he was reluctant to admit it.

"Mornin'." Thor gestured at the fire. The coffeepot sat at the edge of the grill over the flames. "Coffee's just perking. Should be ready in a few minutes."

"That sounds good. I'll be back." Jason stalked off into the forest.

Thor dug out their cups. He added a couple of sticks to the fire. The pot was perking steadily now. He would give it a few more minutes, then pour himself a cup and be out of here.

"Mmm. That smells good," Jason said, holding his empty mug in one hand.

Crouching down, Thor plucked the pot from the heat. He filled Jason's cup, then his own.

"I'm leaving camp for a couple of days." Thor kept his eyes focused on the swirling black liquid in his cup. "We need some supplies, and I need to check on some business." He glanced up.

Jason's brows drew together. "You didn't mention having to leave camp before. I still have lots of pictures to take."

"I figure you can use the next two days to get all the shots around here that you wanted. When I get back we'll spend most of every day out on the mountains. I'll take you over to Bear Mountain and see if we can find some bears. This time of year the raspberries are just starting to ripen. Bears love them." Thor clamped his teeth together to stop himself from chattering like a girl. Jason wasn't stupid. He might catch on to just why he was leaving.

For a few minutes they shared coffee and quiet. Jason seemed to be pondering the situation. As much as he talked about his faith and following God, he might even be praying. That idea really made Thor nervous. He recalled his mother praying for him before she died. Deep inside he always wondered if God told her things about him that no one else knew.

"I thought we brought enough supplies up for the whole two weeks." Jason sipped his coffee, watching Thor through the steam rising from his cup.

"I. . .uh. There are a couple of things I forgot." Thor shifted, rotating his shoulders. He had to leave *now*. He edged toward the truck.

"Whatever you think we need, I'm sure we can do fine without it. I'm used to roughing it." Jason paused. "Is this because of Jazmyn?"

"Jazmyn?" Thor stared at him. How had the man known? He groped for something to say, some way to deny the obvious attraction he felt toward her.

"Yeah. I didn't say for sure that I'd be bringing her. She doesn't need anything special. Before we came up here I told her the food wouldn't be like the corner deli." Jason flashed Thor a grin. "You don't have to treat her different."

Thor took a big gulp of coffee, trying to buy time. He couldn't tell if Jason didn't suspect a thing or was simply trying to give him an out. From the glint in Jason's eye Thor thought he was being teased.

"I didn't intend to get special food for Jazmyn." Thor tried to keep the defensiveness from his voice. "When I brought supplies I thought there would only be two of us. I'll pick up a few things, then check on some business matters with my sister."

Jason nodded, staring into the fire for a few minutes. The sky lightened. Across the river Thor could see a doe taking hesitant steps down to the water. She took a drink. Her head jerked up. Droplets of water scattered from her muzzle. She leaped back into the woods, disappearing into the undergrowth.

"That deer reminds me of Jazmyn."

Thor caught himself before he agreed with Jason. The grace and beauty of the animal took his breath away just as

Jazmyn did, but he didn't want to share that information with her brother. "How so?"

"She's so delicate. I mean that in the emotional sense. She's been hurt. It's hard for her to build a relationship with anyone. She doesn't want to trust them; she wants to run away instead."

Thor wondered if Jason meant him instead of Jazmyn. Wasn't that why he was leaving this morning? Running away? His jaw muscles tightened. He wouldn't run from anything. He needed to go to town.

"She's starting to heal and come out of her shell," Jason continued. "I'd hate to see her hurt so bad she withdraws again." His green eyes, a shade darker than Jazmyn's, met Thor's.

"I'd hate to see her hurt, too." Thor cleared his throat. "I'm taking off. I'll be back day after tomorrow." He strode to the truck, patted the dogs before climbing in, and refused to glance in the rearview mirror as he eased across the river. On the off chance that Jazmyn was up early, he couldn't risk seeing her in tousled disarray. If the urge to protect her, to hold her, to love her rose up again, he didn't know how he could fight it. The best thing for him right now was to put as much distance between himself and that alluring beauty as possible.

On the four-hour drive to his cabin, he berated himself for being weak, for feeling an attraction to another woman after he'd seen how conniving women could be. *I will not fall for this woman. It's just because she's needy and I want to help her out. That's all.*

Although the argument with himself continued for most of the morning, Thor still wondered at his motives. No matter what he did, visions of Jazmyn popped unbidden into his head. All day he wondered what she was doing, wishing he was with her.

❧

Warmth flooded the tent when Jazmyn woke up. Full sunlight

filtered through the canvas, making her blink at the brightness. She yawned and stretched. It was late. Why hadn't Jason awakened her?

She could hear Jason humming as she unzipped the tent and stepped out. The smell of sausage made her stomach grumble. At home she would never dream of eating something as fatty as sausage for breakfast, but out here she couldn't wait to taste it. Jason and Thor were right. Something about the wilderness changed a person's taste in food.

"Mornin'." Jason smiled at her.

"To you, too." Jazmyn glanced around, wondering where Thor was.

"I thought you were going to sleep the whole day." Jason cracked an egg into the skillet.

"Why didn't you get me up? I thought we were going out early to get pictures again." She still didn't see Thor.

"Our guide left before daybreak." Jason avoided her gaze as he flipped the egg.

"He left? Why?" For the first time she noticed Thor's truck wasn't parked in the usual spot. The dogs weren't there to greet her, either.

Jason shrugged. "He said he needed some supplies and had some business to attend to."

"I thought you were his business right now." Jazmyn could feel anger worming up inside her. "He's supposed to be helping you get the photos you need."

"He'll be back day after tomorrow. We'll still have plenty of time for everything. You want breakfast first or a walk in the woods?"

Jazmyn blushed. She still hadn't become accustomed to going off into the woods to take care of her needs. Although she'd only used an outhouse once, and remembered the stench clearly, she would rather have that than just a tree between her and the rest of the world.

"I'll be right back." She headed off through the trees. Embarrassed or not, this was necessity.

By the time she returned, Jason was dishing up potatoes, sausage, and eggs for both of them. "I made you some hot chocolate today instead of coffee." He set the mug on the table. "I thought you might like the change."

Breathing in the spicy chocolate smell, Jazmyn almost purred. "Mmm. If I close my eyes, I can almost imagine there's a hint of cinnamon in here. Thanks." She wrinkled her nose at Jason, a trick they'd done to one another when they were kids. Their parents always got mad if they stuck their tongues out, so Jazmyn and Jason decided this gesture would mean the same to them, but no one else would know.

They prayed and both dug in. "I can't believe how hungry I am." Jazmyn popped a piece of sausage into her mouth. "At home I almost never eat more than a piece of toast for breakfast."

"I know." Jason raised one eyebrow. "You look it, too. I was hoping to fatten you up on this camping trip."

She wrinkled her nose at him again. "Well, if I stay here too long, I can audition for the part of Miss Piggy in the next Muppet movie."

"Nah. You'd never get it. Your hair is too red."

"If it didn't taste so good, I'd throw my breakfast at you," Jazmyn grumbled.

Jason finished his meal and took the dishes over to the dishpan. "I've heated water for dishes. I wondered if you could do them so I can walk downriver and try for some more photos today." He paused and looked at her. "Or would you like to go with me?"

"No way. I've had enough walking for a lifetime. I'll stay here and read or just relax. You go on."

"I think I'll pack a sandwich and some snacks in case I don't make it back by lunch. Don't worry about me, okay?"

"Will you be back in time for supper?" Jazmyn watched as Jason gathered the things he needed. She didn't want to let him know how much she dreaded being alone in camp all day. She'd go with him, but she knew she'd only be a hindrance.

Thirty minutes later she watched as Jason headed toward the river, his camera bag over his shoulder. Part of her wanted to run after him, but the bigger part wanted to stay. She needed time to sort out her feelings about Thor.

When Jason first said Thor had gone to town that morning, she'd been angry. Now she wondered if that wasn't just hurt over the fact that he'd left without saying good-bye. Several times since they'd arrived at camp she'd felt as if Thor were watching her. Had he sensed an attraction between them? She didn't know for sure. Her experience with men was minimal, but a few times she thought he might feel something toward her.

The rest of the morning passed quickly. After doing dishes Jazmyn settled down with her Bible. Studying proved difficult. The chipmunks had invited friends. Four of them now scampered around the camp, nosing into everything.

A big squirrel, her bushy tail waving, paused a few feet from the ground, her claws holding her fast to the trunk of a pine. She stared at Jazmyn with black beady eyes.

Getting a piece of bread, Jazmyn spent an hour throwing crumbs to the chipmunks. The squirrel got into the game, chasing away the smaller animals whenever she could. Jazmyn couldn't help but laugh at their antics. When she tried to interfere on behalf of the chipmunks, the squirrel raced up a tree to a branch overhead. From there she shrieked and chattered at Jazmyn for several minutes.

"I'm sure glad I don't speak squirrel language." Jazmyn

gazed up at the disgruntled animal. "You're such a fighter, I think I'll call you Xena, the warrior squirrel." Xena didn't appear to appreciate her new name as she raced along the branch then stopped and screeched some more.

After lunch Jazmyn decided to take a walk. She'd told Jason she was tired of walking, but the truth was she needed time to think. She couldn't understand why Thor would leave so suddenly. Had she said something? Done something?

"Watch the camp, Xena." Jazmyn scribbled a quick note for Jason, picked up a long stick, and started up a faint trail. Maybe she could get to the top of this hill and see if there was a view.

eight

"This is so stupid," Thor growled to the dogs, which were riding in the cab this time. "I can't stand to be there. I can't stand to be away. This is stupid." Loki leaned close and licked him on the chin. "Yeah, I know. I said that before."

He almost had to yell as the truck rattled down the dirt road leading back to camp. The late afternoon sun hung low in the sky. A herd of deer startled in the forest as he rounded a corner.

He hadn't been able to stay away a full day. He'd no sooner arrived at his cabin than he realized he had to go back. Guiding was his job and a serious responsibility, he told himself. How could he let a customer down like that? So he checked a couple of business matters, packed up the dogs, and left. After a quick stop at a store for a few special items, he began the long journey back to the mountain camp.

Clouds were building in the distance as Thor slowed for the river crossing. A faint rumble of thunder echoed from the distance. He could see Jason's SUV now. His pulse sped up. It was the knowledge that he was taking care of his responsibility, he told himself. This wasn't excitement at the thought of seeing Jazmyn again. Besides, he didn't need to align himself with another gold digger, and, as he well knew, most women were gold diggers, his mother and sister excepted.

A few minutes later he stepped out of the truck. The dogs piled out after him, racing from one end of the camp to the other. They were glad to be back.

"Hello," he called, expecting to see Jason or Jazmyn by the

fire. There was no fire. It had gone out during the day, and no one had kept it up. A frisson of unease swept through him. Where were they?

Thor slammed the truck door shut and turned to study the river. Maybe they had gone for a walk before starting supper.

Loki and Odin trotted up, begging for attention. He rubbed their heads as his gaze wandered across the clearings and through the underbrush.

"Well, boys, I guess I should make myself useful. Let's get that fire going and get some supper started. They'll be hungry when they get back." Thor pushed back irritation at not seeing Jazmyn first thing when he arrived at camp. For all she and Jason knew he wouldn't be back for at least another day.

He had the fire blazing when Jason stumbled from the wooded path leading to the river. The man looked scared and exhausted. When he spotted Thor he stopped and stared, but no smile lit his face.

"Jason, you okay?" Thor put the meat back in the cooler and walked over to where Jason stood zombie-like. "Where's Jazmyn?"

Jason shook his head. His mouth opened and shut like some marionette trying to speak. He took a deep breath and shuddered. "I can't find her."

"What?" Thor wanted to shake the man. "What do you mean you can't find her?"

Jason ran a hand through his hair. "I left this morning to walk the river downstream and get some pictures. When I got back this afternoon I found a note from Jazmyn saying she'd gone for a walk."

Thor relaxed. "She's probably on her way back then. She'll be getting hungry. . ."

"You don't understand. Jazmyn hates exercise. Remember how she complained about all the walking we were doing? If she went for a walk, she would have been back within a half-hour or so. I've been back for two hours, and she still hasn't returned."

Thor thought about the times he and Jason had taken Jazmyn out for the photo shoots. She had complained about the walking and her muscles aching. In fact, her hatred of exercise had gotten to be a joke between them.

"Look, I know she's not downstream. That's where I was." Jason gestured in the direction of the river. "I went upstream quite a ways looking for her and calling. I couldn't find any sign of her passing, either."

Thor's gaze strayed to the steep hillside behind him. He could almost hear what Jason was thinking. "If she's gone to find the top of the mountain, she could be anywhere by now." He felt heavy with dread. What he left unsaid, but knew Jason was also thinking, was the number of times people got lost this way. They thought it would be easy to walk to the top of the mountain, but the top was over a series of rises, not just straight up. After they went over a couple of small peaks, inexperienced hikers couldn't tell where they'd come up so they could return the same way.

"I'll head up and look for her," Thor said.

"I'm going, too."

"No." He stopped, noting the harshness of his voice and the effect it had on Jason. "You've been hiking all day. You're tired. Stay here. Get some supper cooking. She'll be hungry when I bring her back."

"Okay." Jason nodded. "You'll need some water."

"Get the jacket I loaned her. It might be in her tent." Thor glanced up at the sky. It was already cooling off. He didn't have much time. Grabbing a flashlight from behind the truck seat, he whistled to the dogs.

"I'll take Odin with me. He has the best nose." He grabbed

the pack Jason handed him, knowing there would be water and food inside.

"I'll be praying." Jason's words followed Thor into the woods. Thor's mother always told him that, too.

Odin began to cast from side to side after sniffing at a shirt of Jazmyn's. Thor had noted where a small trail led up the hill. If he were an inexperienced person like Jazmyn, that's where he would head. He whistled. Odin trotted over. The dog sniffed the ground, the snuffling sound familiar and comforting to Thor. If any dog could find Jazmyn, it was Odin. He only hoped they found her before it was too late. So many things could happen to someone alone in the mountains.

A sharp bark caught his attention. Odin glanced up at him then trotted off up the mountain, his nose testing the air. Thor followed after him, wishing he knew how to pray like Jason and his mother. Fear for Jazmyn's safety threatened to consume him instead.

❧

Jazmyn's legs ached with the strain of climbing the hill. She paused to catch her breath. Far below she could still see the glint of the river through the mass of trees. Looking up she could see the crest of the rise not far away. "Who'd ever guess going uphill could be so tiring?"

An outcropping of white rocks covered with dry moss stood in her way. Skirting them would take too much time, so she found the best way up and scrambled over the rough surface. When she looked back down she'd lost sight of the river. That didn't worry her. All she had to do was head back down. Their camp lay straight below her.

Reaching the crest, she groaned aloud. This wasn't the top of the mountain but only a little dip leading to another part of the hill. She debated going back down, but a glance at her watch told her Jason wouldn't be back for a while. She didn't want to sit by herself in the camp for hours.

"May as well try to find the top while I'm this far." She started up again, walking more slowly than before. Halfway up the next section she came to another bunch of rocks. This time she went far enough to one side to avoid so much climbing. Her hands still hurt from the last rocks she went over.

Several times Jazmyn thought sure she would reach the peak, only to find another ridge to navigate. She had to work her way around fallen trees and huge boulders. When she finally reached what she thought had to be the top of the mountain, Jazmyn groaned. Another false lead. A low flat rock stuck out like the outcropping in the *Lion King* movie. With the last of her strength she pulled herself up and lay down gasping for breath.

"Why am I killing myself like this?" Her whole body ached so badly she wanted to cry. She wouldn't be able to move for a week.

It was a moot question. She knew deep down she wanted the physical pain to override her emotional pain. Thor's leaving had hurt. Her mother's voice echoed in her head. "Men are all alike. They lie to you and then leave you." She pushed the thought away.

"I don't even want a relationship with him, Lord, so why am I hurting? He's not a Christian, and I'm committed to following You." Tears burned her eyes.

Last night as she lay in her sleeping bag, she determined not to have as much to do with Thor. She thought about how scared of him she'd been when she first met him and couldn't believe how mistaken she'd been. He wasn't some cruel killer. He had compassion and cared for people. How many times had Thor come to her defense when Jason teased her? She couldn't count them all.

This morning when she found out he was gone, her heart

began to ache. She felt responsible, as if he wanted to be away from her. This afternoon she didn't know any more about why he'd gone, but she knew she missed him. Missed him more than she had a right to.

She must have dropped off to sleep on the warm rock. When she woke up shadows were darkening under the trees. Sitting up, she rubbed her eyes. She'd better get back before Jason got worried about her.

Hopping off the rock, Jazmyn staggered. Her aching muscles had seized up as she rested. They were screaming at her now. She groaned as she stretched her legs out. At least going back would be all downhill. Going straight down shouldn't take long.

She was wrong. Straight down proved almost harder on her legs than walking uphill. Each step jarred her muscles. When she reached the bottom she stared around in amazement. Where was the river? She should be able to see it from here or at least hear the water. She couldn't hear a thing except the birds twittering overhead. She couldn't see much, either. The shadows had thickened among the trees.

Across a small ravine the hill rose up again. Jazmyn knew she hadn't come this way, yet to get back to camp she'd only had to go downhill. Hadn't she? She sank to the ground as she thought about all the times she'd gone around trees and rocks. At the time she was sure she wasn't changing course. Now she began to wonder.

She rested her forehead on her knees. "Okay, think, Jazmyn. There has to be a way out of this." She closed her eyes and pictured the mountains as she'd seen them from the lookout they stopped at yesterday on the way back to camp. The tree-covered hills seemed to roll on forever. No one lived near here. If she got lost, she might never be found.

Panic tightened her chest, threatening to cut off her breath.

Rubbing her arms, she tried to ignore the chill racing through her. She didn't have a jacket or any food. She hadn't said in the note exactly where she'd be hiking. Jason would have no idea where to look for her. Thor wouldn't be back for two days, so he couldn't help. She hadn't even brought water.

She swiped at the tears trickling down her cheeks. She wouldn't survive the night. Before long some bear or mountain lion would be out hunting and smell her. How could she hope to fight a creature like that?

Fear washed over her. Sinking onto her side, she rolled into a tight ball. All the years with her mother came rushing back. She could hear her mother scolding her about the dangers of the outside world. "Stay away from men. They'll do nothing but lead you into trouble and then leave you to deal with it." Her mother's bitter voice rang in her ears.

"God, help me." The whisper startled her. She hadn't thought to pray. Why did prayer come so easy to Jason, while she always thought about it as a last resort?

Pushing against the ground, she sat back up. "God, I'm lost. You know where I am, though. You know how afraid I am. Please, Lord, help me to be strong. Help me to know what to do."

Keeping her eyes closed, Jazmyn assessed her options. She could go back up to the top of the mountain. However, if she tried that, she might end up on another mountaintop and be even more lost.

She could try to walk around this hill and see if she could find a road or the river. Another option was to wait right here. Maybe Jason would find her soon. A sob caught in her throat. How would he ever do that? Besides, if she tried walking in the dark, she might fall off some ridge.

Something crashed in the brush up the mountain. Jazmyn jumped. She scrambled to her feet, staring uphill. She squinted, trying to see through the shadowy dimness.

A rock skittered down. Taking a step back, she glanced from side to side, trying to find some sort of shelter. The trees were too tall to climb. Besides, a bear or cougar could climb up after her.

Brush rattled. Something big was coming down the hill—fast. She began to tremble. Should she shout? Her vocal cords refused to work. Should she run? Her legs wouldn't move. Paralyzing fear froze her to the spot as she waited for the end.

Before she could scream, something broke through the brush and hurtled into the air. She opened her mouth, but the breath was knocked out of her as the beast hit her in the chest, knocking her backward to the ground. This was the end. Any moment now her throat would be ripped out.

nine

Something warm and wet slopped across her chin. Jazmyn waited for the fatal bite. She could feel warm breath on her face.

"Either eat her or let her up, Odin."

Her eyes flew open. Odin lay on her chest looking very pleased with himself. She turned her head to see Thor squatting beside her. The corners of his eyes crinkled with mirth. She burst into tears.

"Hey, you're supposed to be happy to see us." Thor shoved Odin off her and lifted Jazmyn to her feet as if she weighed nothing. He wrapped his arms around her. She clung to him, all her earlier resolve to keep her distance fading away.

The hike back to camp passed in a blur. Darkness settled in. Thor's flashlight was almost strong enough to power New York City. Odin leaped and cavorted around them for a few minutes then settled into the seriousness of leading them in the right direction.

Jason had supper on when they arrived. Jazmyn could see the relief in his eyes. She was too tired to talk and ended up in bed long before either of the men was ready to let her out of his sight. They'd become very protective. Her last thought before falling asleep was to wonder how Thor came to rescue her when he was supposed to be gone for two days.

Jazmyn almost cried when she tried to climb out of her sleeping bag the next morning. She recalled reading somewhere that the human body has over six hundred muscles. Every one of hers was making its presence known today.

"Mornin', Jaz." Jason grinned as she limped over to him.

"Today I mixed the coffee and hot chocolate for you. Mocha java, I guess." He handed her a steaming mug. She almost kissed him.

Thor leaned against the table, studying her as he sipped his coffee. Morning light hadn't yet touched the sky. "Today we're going to a place that requires a lot of hiking. I'm not sure you should go with us. We'll be gone most of the day."

"I can wait in the truck while you're getting the pictures." Jazmyn could feel panic welling up. She didn't want to be left in camp again.

"Sis, just riding in the truck over rough roads will hurt. You've got to be sore. I watched you walk over here. You need to wait here."

"We'll be back by mid-afternoon, I hope. I've packed some sandwiches." Thor looked as if he wanted to say more but didn't. "Go back to bed. Get some more rest."

I will not be afraid. Jazmyn gritted her teeth and fought to swallow the lump in her throat.

"I have something for you." Jason set down his cup and went to the SUV. He rummaged around for a few minutes and came back carrying a large bag. "I brought this in case you had some time on your hands."

Taking the sack from him, Jazmyn waited for the joke. Jason picked up his cup and watched her. Thor looked curious. He did not know what was going on. Inside the bag were several drawing pencils and two artist's pads. She blinked to clear her eyes.

Jazmyn loved to draw. When she met Adam he encouraged her to do more than doodle on the edges of paper. During the years they dated she found a lot of comfort when she sat down to draw. Sketching came naturally to her, and Adam loved to watch her. When he died her desire to continue with her art died with him.

Her gaze met Jason's. She knew what he was saying. It was time to put Adam behind her. She had to move on with her life. Jason had tried to say this before, but she hadn't been ready to hear. For some reason, she thought she might be ready now.

In the flickering light of the lantern, she smiled at Jason. "Thanks. I think I might try this."

A look of profound relief crossed Jason's face. She thought of all the times he'd expressed concern over her continued pining for Adam. He'd wanted her to see a counselor. In fact, he'd set up an appointment with a counselor from his church, but she didn't want to talk to some stranger about her problems, especially when she didn't share that person's beliefs.

Her life had spiraled from there. Jason left town on a photo shoot for a new book. When he returned three months later, Jazmyn had almost become a recluse. Jason took her under his wing, saying he wouldn't leave her again until she was strong enough. Then he told her about Jesus and the strength and peace she would get from knowing Him.

Many times Jason had talked to her about God. Other times she'd laughed, but this time she was ready to listen. Her life turned upside down at that point but not for the worse. She was still learning to change, to accept.

She waved as Jason and Thor drove away. The last of her mocha coffee had cooled. She set the cup on the table and limped back to her tent. Thor's idea of getting a little more sleep sounded like a winner.

By the time she got up again, the sun was well overhead. She took a short walk along the river, careful not to lose sight of the camp. The movement seemed to relieve some of the soreness in her muscles.

❧

Pulling a chair under the shade of the tarp, Jazmyn opened the bag Jason had given her, retrieving the pencils and drawing pad. After putting some bread crumbs on a rock, she waited for the squirrels and chipmunks to show up. The day passed in a blur as she lost herself in sketching. She'd forgotten how restful this could be.

Taking a break, Jazmyn rummaged in the supplies and found a chocolate bar. She settled back into her chair, broke off a chunk, and set the rest of the candy on the table beside her.

Her thoughts strayed to Thor. She couldn't deny the way her pulse sped up when she saw him this morning. The sight of him brought back the memory of him holding her last night. She'd felt so safe and comforted. When he carried her part of the way back to camp, she wanted to stay in his arms forever.

Lord, these feelings are so dangerous. I know that. Please show me what to do. Am I turning to him as a comfort when I should be turning to You? I don't want to do that.

Picking up her Bible, Jazmyn turned to the verse in 2 Timothy Jason had showed her. She read it again. "For God hath not given us the spirit of fear; but of power, and of love, and of a sound mind." *Lord, if these fears aren't from You, then show me how to get rid of them.*

Without looking, she reached for the rest of her candy bar on the table. Her hand met fur. She shrieked and jumped up. Her chair tumbled sideways. Xena the squirrel raced away with the candy bar in her mouth.

"Hey, come back here! That's mine." Jazmyn gave chase. Xena scampered up a tree, the wide bar held in her teeth. As Jazmyn raced over, Xena lost her hold on the candy. The chocolate fell to the ground. Xena leaped onto a limb several feet above Jazmyn and almost vibrated with anger. Jazmyn had to laugh as Xena screeched her outrage over losing the treat.

❧

The sun was setting as Thor sped down the gravel road taking him and Jason back to camp. Dust spiraled up behind them. He knew that if a Forest Service ranger found him going this fast, his goose would be cooked, but he wanted to get back to camp. They were three hours later than they had planned to be. All he could think about was the panic that consumed him when Jazmyn was lost in the woods. He knew from the silence that Jason felt the same.

The hike had gone well. They'd found a flock of turkeys, an eagle, and an eagle's nest. Jazmyn would have enjoyed the wildlife, but the hiking was brutal. Besides, she would have fainted from fright watching him hold Jason's legs while Jason dangled over the cliff edge for pictures.

Rounding a curve, the tail of the pickup slid sideways. Thor swung the wheel in the direction of the slide, and the truck straightened out. Trees flashed past. Open meadows spread out on one side and then the other. Sparkling streams meandered through the woods. He ignored the beauty of the mountains he loved as his mind strayed to the previous night.

When he followed Odin into the forest after Jazmyn, fear held him captive. For the first time ever he wished he had the faith of his mother so he could pray and get help from somewhere. Would God even bother to answer a prayer like that? He wasn't sure. Thor always prided himself on his ability to care for himself and others. He didn't need any God.

Last night had come close to changing that opinion. What if he didn't find Jazmyn in time? She was always so afraid of everything. How could she cope in a darkening world when she didn't know what to do to protect herself? All those thoughts had raced through his mind as he let Odin lead him farther up the mountain.

When they found Jazmyn, he'd forgotten the need for God. He could take things from there. God surely had other things to tend to, didn't He? What was it Jason had said a couple of weeks ago when they met to discuss the trip? Something about God caring about every part of your life and wanting to be involved in every decision. That was a little too one-on-one for Thor. He would prefer a God who stepped up when needed, not one who meddled all the time.

"Looks like we'll have a late supper," Jason said as they neared the river crossing. "I can get the fire and lanterns going while you fix the meal."

"Deal." Thor's stomach churned. He didn't feel like food until he found out whether Jazmyn was okay. "Aren't you worried about your sister? You've been so quiet."

Jason gave him a tired smile. "I've been praying. That way I don't have to worry. I know God is handling everything."

"You mean you weren't worried last night?"

"No, I'm human," Jason admitted. "I was worried today, but I'm not now. Even when things don't go like I wanted them to, I know I can trust God's plan. If He's going to be my God, then I have to give Him all my life and let Him run everything. If I take something back by worrying or wanting control in some other way, I'm saying He's not good enough to be my God."

Jason's words struck Thor hard. Wasn't that the way he treated God? Like some tool he used only when he thought he needed Him. *Let me live my life the way I want, God, but be there in case I mess up and need You to bail me out.* That was his philosophy so far. Look how messed up his life had become.

Water sprayed up as Thor drove into the river faster than he should have. He switched on the wipers to clear the windshield. Flames were shooting up from a big fire in the fire pit at camp. Someone had either kept the fire going or gotten it started again tonight. Another concern sprang up to clench his stomach. Who had been in camp with Jazmyn while they were gone?

"I can't believe it," Jason said. "My sister kept the fire going."

"You sure?" Thor squinted, trying to see any other vehicles around the camp.

"There she is adding another log." Jason laughed. "If we don't stop her, she'll have a fire big enough to burn whole trees."

Jazmyn waved as they pulled to a stop in the usual spot. The dogs leaped to their feet and bounded over to the truck. Thor and Jason both hopped out.

The first thing Thor noticed was the smell. Someone had been cooking, and it smelled good.

"About time." Jazmyn stretched up and gave Jason a peck on the cheek. "I thought you were doing a night photo shoot."

"I came back here for that." Jason gave her a hug. "What smells so good?"

She smiled. "I thought you might be hungry, so I started some supper."

"I hope it's done. I'm hungry enough to eat one of these trees." Jason reached over and broke off a piece of bark, which he stuck in his mouth. He rolled his eyes and made sounds of delight. Thor couldn't help laughing.

"Stop that." Jazmyn plucked the piece of bark from Jason's mouth. "You don't know what animal may have been climbing that tree." She tried to give him a fierce look but ended up grinning.

"Let me put up my camera equipment and wash up. Then I'll be ready to eat."

Thor watched Jazmyn as she turned to look at him. She hesitated as if she wasn't sure she wanted to be around him. He understood. He didn't know how to act around her, either.

"So, what's on the menu?" he asked. "Anything I can help with?"

She shrugged. "I got the stove started like you showed me." She tried not to show her pride, but he could hear it in her voice. "I have some fried potatoes, pork chops, and peas ready to eat. I hope that's all right."

"That's my favorite meal." She was close enough to touch. He had to fight the urge. "I have to admit I'm amazed you did this, plus keep the fire going."

She glanced at the flames. "God is changing me. Last night He showed me I don't have to be afraid. I can depend on Him to help me out no matter what."

"I need to wash." Thor stalked away. Why did God keep coming up all the time?

ten

"What are you doing?" Jazmyn stared at Jason as he stood near the fire. The morning sun cast its first feeble rays across the treetops.

"I'm having breakfast." Jason frowned at her, a look reminiscent of his childhood.

"You can't have that for breakfast." She put her hands on her hips and wondered if she sounded like their mother.

"Why not? Will the parent police come after me?"

"It's not healthy, you know."

"So what is around here?" Jason stuffed another marshmallow on a stick and held it over the flames. "Besides, this is our last day. I've used all my film, and I'm celebrating."

"But s'mores?" She gave a mock shudder.

Thor emerged as Jason pulled the perfect brown marshmallow from the fire. "Ah, you're fixing breakfast." He plucked the crispy treat from the end of the stick, stuck it between two graham crackers with chocolate, and bit off a huge bite.

Jason's mouth fell open. "Hey, that was mine."

Thor stuffed the rest in his mouth, his cheeks bulging. "Ou won it ack?" Jazmyn held her sides as she laughed at Jason's expression. Her brother wasn't used to anyone getting one over on him.

"All right, so I haven't done my share of the cooking." Jason grabbed two more marshmallows from the bag. "I'm fixing breakfast for us all."

Thor bowed to Jazmyn and gestured to a chair near the fire. "Have a seat, my lady. This knave will have your meal fixed in a few moments."

She spread her fingers in front of her face as if they were a fan. "My knight. Thank you."

Thor's mouth twitched. "Anything for my lady." He led her to the chair and held her arm as she sat down.

"All right, you two, enough of the theatrics. I'm thinking we should leave for home now. I may not be able to stand the two of you all day." Jason shoved a s'more at Jazmyn. "Breakfast is served."

"Watch out." Jazmyn pointed behind him.

Jason swung around as Xena skittered over to the box of chocolate. She bared her teeth and raised her tail.

"Be careful, Jason. She has this thing for chocolate." Jazmyn tried to smother a laugh.

Jason waved his hands at her. "Shoo. Get out of here."

Xena raised up on her hind legs and stared at him with her black beady eyes. She took a hop closer. Jason took a step. Xena leaped on the box and shrieked at Jason.

"Hey, she's vicious!" Jason called over his shoulder.

"You can tell she's a female by the way she's willing to fight for her chocolate." Thor grinned.

"Hey, I resent that." Jazmyn tried her best to stare daggers in Thor's direction. She and Thor looked at each other and started to laugh. Xena skittered up the tree, scolding them from a branch above.

The day sped by. Jazmyn watched as Thor and Jason took down any extra tarps they wouldn't need so there would be less to do tomorrow. She tried to ignore the heaviness that weighted her. When she'd first arrived at camp, she hadn't wanted to be here. She thought the two weeks would be interminable. Now that it was time to leave, she didn't want to return to the hot city and her nowhere job. The mountains had grown on her. She wanted to stay. Even the quiet had grown on her.

As evening drew near, a doe stepped out of the trees. Jazmyn reached for her pad and pencil. She had drawn plenty of chipmunks and squirrels, but this was the first time a deer had come close enough to sketch. She prayed the guys would stay quiet long enough for her to complete the sketch.

Her pencil flew over the paper. At the light scratching sound, the deer's ear, twitched. Her large brown eyes stared at Jazmyn. She took a hesitant step and bolted into the trees, her white tail flicking up as she ran.

"You know, you're really good," Thor said as he looked over her shoulder. A shiver ran through her. She clutched the pencil and pad, wanting to hide her work but knowing it was too late.

"I didn't get finished before she left."

"Well, it looks perfect to me. What's wrong with it?"

"I didn't get her stance just right." Jazmyn tilted her head, studying the drawing. "Instead of a picture perfect, it's a picture imperfect."

"Ah. Kind of like life, huh?" Jason spoke up from her other side.

Jazmyn wrinkled her brow. "What?"

"You know. We all want the picture-perfect life. Perfect spouse. Perfect kids. Perfect job. Perfect house." Jason shrugged. "Then we find out that life isn't that way. We aren't perfect, and neither is this world."

Jazmyn nodded. "You're right."

Thor held out his hand. "Can I look at your other sketches?"

She took a deep breath. Sharing her pictures was like sharing a part of herself, and that was hard to do. Adam had encouraged her drawing but saw it as a hobby. She passed the pad of paper to Thor.

He pulled up a chair beside her and thumbed through the notebook. Jazmyn wanted to run away. The Scripture she'd read in Psalms yesterday flashed through her thoughts: "I sought the LORD, and He heard me, and delivered me from all my fears." Peace settled over her as she watched Thor turn the pages.

"These are really good." He glanced up at Jason. "Have you considered having her do some illustrations for the book you're working on? You know, these could emphasize the photos and make them stand out more." He was pointing to a sketch of the chipmunks playing on a rock.

Jason moved to Thor's side. "I hadn't thought of that, but you're right. I'll talk to my editor about using them. Do you mind, Jaz?"

"I don't know." She wasn't sure she was ready to have other people look at her drawings. What if they weren't that good?

"Jazmyn, these are very good." Thor spoke as if he'd been reading her thoughts. "I can almost see these creatures coming to life. What will it hurt to try?"

"Hey, you've been unhappy with your work situation for some time," Jason said. "Maybe this will provide an income and give you some variety, too."

⁂

Watching the emotions flit across Jazmyn's face, Thor found himself wanting to make the decision for her. He'd never seen such realistic renditions of the animals in the mountains. The chipmunks and squirrels she'd drawn looked as if they could leap off the page at a moment's notice. She had more artistic talent than most of the people employed in that department of his company.

He would have to consider his options here. He didn't want Jazmyn to know he was anything more than a backwoods hunting guide, yet he wanted her to have the opportunity to use her talents. Handing the pad back to her, he mumbled something about needing to start supper and walked away to think.

Supper was a silent affair. Thor detected a sadness in Jazmyn and wondered if she would miss the mountains. She'd changed so much in the past two weeks. She'd become more confident and less fearful. In short, she'd blossomed. He liked the change. He liked her. A lot.

Jason had the fire blazing by the time Thor and Jazmyn finished cleaning up the kitchen. The warmth proved welcome as the evening chill settled in. They all pulled up chairs around the fire.

"Do you think it's okay to have s'mores twice in one day?" Jason gave Jazmyn a puppy dog look that made her smile.

"Only if Xena is asleep." She looked over her shoulder at the tree where the squirrel lived.

"Squirrels don't usually come out this late," Thor said. "However, that one might make an exception if she smells chocolate."

"I'll make sure I'm well-armed first." Jason got up to get the needed supplies.

The gooey treats tasted even better than they had that morning. Jazmyn, who hadn't done well with roasting marshmallows, sacrificed four of them to the flames before she got one to stay on her stick. The white sticky masses bubbled at the edge of the coals.

Thor finished his dessert and got up to move the lanterns closer to them. Going over to the table, he found Jazmyn's pad and pencils. He brought them to her, making sure the light fell right so she'd be able to see to draw. She raised an eyebrow in question as he handed the drawing implements to her.

"I noticed our friends over there." He gestured toward the river where a white and black tail waved in the weeds. "I didn't see any sketches of skunks. If they come close, maybe you could do a couple of them for Jason's book."

"You don't give up, do you? My pitiful drawings would

never be good enough for a book." She stared at the skunks wandering through the undergrowth. "You are right, though. I don't have any sketches of them."

Before long the mother skunk and her two babies made their way around the fire pit, snuffling in the dirt. The babies clambered up on the rocks close to the flames.

"Won't their feet get burned?" Jazmyn kept her voice to a whisper as if afraid to startle them.

"If they get hot, I assume they'll climb down." Thor flashed her a grin.

"Look." He nodded his head toward the fire.

One of the baby skunks was teetering on a rock, its tiny paw reaching for a mass of melted white goo. Its brother or sister scurried over to see what the first one was reaching for. Their noses twitched; their eyes shone in the firelight.

"You'd better get busy drawing, or you're gonna miss this one," Thor said. "If I had a camera, I'd take a picture." Her eyes met his, melting his insides like one of her sacrificed marshmallows. "But I'd rather have one of your sketches to hang on my wall."

Jazmyn's pencil began to fly across the page. She didn't even seem to be aware that she'd started sketching. Thor quit watching the skunks and stared, fascinated, at the way the pair were coming to life on the paper. Who would have thought someone could do so much with just a pencil and paper? He couldn't even draw a stick figure.

Jazmyn drew in a sharp breath.

"Sis, you'd better stay still. Mama's here to see what's going on," Jason said.

Glancing down, Thor saw the mother skunk's tail partially wrapped around Jazmyn's leg as she paused to watch her babies. Jazmyn's face had paled. Her pencil stilled.

"Don't worry about her," he whispered. "She's not upset,

just checking on her little ones."

Jazmyn flashed him a smile then turned back to her drawing. The mother waddled over to the fire pit and sniffed the warm rocks. Jazmyn flipped the page and started a new picture. Thor was entranced.

"You know, last spring I guided a group of men from a company called T.L. Enterprises. They were talking about how hard it is to find someone with an artistic bent to design computer pages for their products." Jazmyn and Jason both looked at him. Thor tried to keep his tone casual.

"You might try looking them up. With your experience on the computer and your drawing ability, they might hire you."

Jason nodded. "I've heard of them. They say the owner is a recluse and very eccentric."

"Could be." Thor tried to act nonchalant. "It's something to think about."

Later, as he lay in his sleeping bag, his hands behind his head, Thor couldn't get Jazmyn off his mind. Tomorrow she would disappear from his life. He didn't know how he could bear that. Despite his resolve never to get involved with another woman, this one had gotten under his skin and into his heart.

eleven

Standing outside the huge building in the late summer heat, Jazmyn tried to convince herself that the warmth of the afternoon caused the trickle of sweat down her back. The truth was, she was terrified. All those Scriptures she'd memorized on fear and God's protective strength disappeared from her mind when she looked at this imposing façade.

T.L. Enterprises. A huge company. Much bigger than she'd thought, or she never would have agreed to apply for a job here. After Thor's recommendation of the place, Jason hadn't let up until she sent in her résumé. Within two weeks she'd been called for this interview. Her legs shook.

Air conditioning blasted her as she opened the door and walked into the lobby. After the intense heat outdoors, the building felt cold. Jazmyn wished she'd worn a jacket with her skirt and top.

She relaxed a little as the doors hissed shut, blocking the noise outside. She hadn't realized how loud the city sounds could be until she returned from the mountains. Many times she'd longed for that peace and quiet again.

Two security guards behind a circular desk in the lobby looked up when she came in. The younger one gave her a smile and a nod that told her she looked okay.

"Good morning. Can we help you?" His name badge said Mulligan.

"I have an appointment this morning." Jazmyn clenched her purse, trying not to look as nervous as she felt.

Mulligan stared at her as the older guard, Landers, pulled

out a clipboard with a sheet of paper on it. "With whom?" He studied her as he waited.

"It's with a Kirsten. . ." Jazmyn fumbled in her purse. How could she have forgotten the woman's name? These men would think her an idiot. Tugging the paper free, she held it up. "Kirsten Barnes."

Both guards acted surprised. "Your name?" the older one asked.

"Jazmyn Rondell." She tried not to fidget as Landers picked up a phone and punched in some numbers.

"You'll need to wear this." Mulligan handed her a clip-on badge. He pointed toward a wall on the far side of the lobby. "Take the elevator to the tenth floor. Someone will meet you and take you to Mrs. Barnes's office. She's waiting for you."

Incapable of speech, Jazmyn nodded her thanks to the guards. Her shoes clacked so loudly on the tile floor they almost drowned out the pounding of her heart. As the elevator doors shut, she closed her eyes. "God has not given me a spirit of fear." She repeated the words until the elevator slid to a halt at the tenth floor.

The doors swished open. Jazmyn found herself face-to-face with a beautiful blonde. The woman's hair curved under her chin, the cut the envy of any model. Her bright blue eyes sparkled as she smiled. She had delicate, pixie features.

"You must be Jazmyn. I'm Kirsten Barnes. Welcome to T.L. Enterprises." She took Jazmyn's hand in a firm grip.

Jazmyn was awed by the beauty of the lobby on this floor. A glass curtain wall looked out over the city, while the rest of the room was done in a gray-white that muted the brilliance of the sun. Enlarged photos of the outdoors made her long to be back in the mountains. Several vases and hand-woven baskets rested on pedestals around the room.

"My office is this way." Kirsten led her into a lavish office and gestured to a set of comfortable chairs. Jazmyn slid into one, expecting Kirsten to sit at the massive desk. Instead, the woman took the seat next to hers.

Another woman entered the office from a side door carrying a serving tray. She smiled at Jazmyn as she set the tray on the table in front of them.

"Jazmyn, this is my assistant, Madeline Henry. If you come to work here, you'll get to know her. Some people call her mad, but her friends call her Maddy."

Maddy winked at Jazmyn. "Kirsten is the one who spreads the rumor about me being mad. She thinks that way no one will steal me away from her." With a saucy shake of her head, the young woman left the room.

Kirsten shook her head and sighed. "She is right about one thing. I don't know what I'd do if someone stole her away from me. She's invaluable." She lifted a cup and gestured to the tray. "Would you like tea or coffee?"

Her mouth dry, Jazmyn tried to swallow. Kirsten seemed so nice, but Jazmyn had never been good at meeting people. "Coffee, please." She prayed she wouldn't rattle the cup with her shaking hands.

"I love coffee, too." Kirsten poured, placing the cup on the table in front of Jazmyn. "I see Maddy has provided some sweets. Would you like those now or after the interview?"

"I think later." Jazmyn cleared her throat, hoping Kirsten hadn't noticed the squeak in her voice.

Whatever she'd expected, this interview was like nothing she could have imagined. Kirsten treated her more like a friend, wanting to get to know her better. By degrees, Jazmyn managed to relax. By the time she finished her coffee, she and Kirsten were laughing about the camping trip and Xena the warrior squirrel.

"I haven't been camping in years," Kirsten said. "The last

time I did any camping, my brothers dangled a snake from the awning over the tent. When I ducked out the next morning, I came face-to-face with the creepy thing. They said my scream scared off all the animals in the forest." She shuddered. "I still don't like tents. If I went camping again, I would have to sleep in a luxury camper with no awning and no brothers in sight."

Jazmyn laughed and waited for Kirsten to get down to the business of interviewing her. She was surprised when the woman said, "So, when can you start?"

Jazmyn almost choked. "You mean I have the job? I mean, I can start anytime."

"This is Friday," Kirsten said. "How about starting Monday? I can have your badge made up and all the paperwork done this afternoon." She smiled. "I did tell you Maddy is a miracle worker, didn't I?"

Jazmyn could only nod. She listened in silence as Kirsten explained the job description to her. Jazmyn would need to put in a certain amount of hours, but after the training period she could set her own schedule. This job was like a dream come true.

❧

Thor drummed his fingers on his desk as he waited for his brother to answer the phone. Most people thought of his cabin in the mountains as an antiquated shack. They hadn't seen this back room. In fact, no one other than his brother had been in here.

This room was where he ran his business. He had all the modern conveniences here. He kept in constant touch with his sister, Kirsten, and his brother, Erik. The fact that they were his half-sister and half-brother had no meaning to him. They'd always considered themselves family growing up, and nothing had changed now. They would do anything for each other. Thor appreciated the way they conducted the hands-on running of his company so he could maintain his distance.

"You're hiding away," Kirsten would accuse him. "You can't stay up on that mountain all your life. You need to meet a decent woman and get married."

Since Kirsten had met her husband, Wes Barnes, she'd decided everyone should be married and happy like she was. Thor didn't believe that was possible. He'd had too many narrow misses with shallow women to want to try meeting any more of them. So why was he so interested in Jazmyn Rondell?

For the last few weeks since he returned from that camping trip, he'd been checking into her. He knew everything he could possibly learn about Jazmyn. He told his siblings he was doing a background check because he wanted to know if she would be a good future employee of T.L. Enterprises. That was a lie. He wanted to know her because she intrigued him. He couldn't get her out of his mind.

"Peterson."

"About time," Thor snapped at his brother. "I thought you were taking a nap."

Erik heaved an exaggerated sigh over the phone. "What is it this time, Thor? It's been five whole minutes since we last talked."

"Um. I wondered about. . ."

"I know. You want to know about the interview. Kirsten is still at work. When she gets home, I promise to have her call you."

"No." Thor could feel the sweat bead on his forehead. "I'm just interested in a new employee, that's all."

"Right." Erik snorted. "You've never bugged us before about a simple interview. Of course, you've never told Kirsten whom to hire for what before, either. Would you like me to pop out and get a ring? I could go right in and end the interview with a proposal from you. I'm sure that would be appropriate."

"Very funny, Erik."

"Listen, Thor. Kirsten has her work, and I'm trying to get some things done for my trip tomorrow. Why don't you come to town? Spend a few days at the house. You can see for yourself how Jazmyn is doing."

"I can't do that." Thor could hear a note of panic in his voice. "I. . .um. I have some work to do here." He could almost see Erik drumming his fingers on the desk waiting for the truth. "I can't let her know who I am."

Erik's tone softened. "You have to get over the past, Thor. If this woman is worth what you think, then your status won't matter."

"I know. I will tell her." He rubbed his forehead. "I'll tell her soon."

"Listen, I'll have Kirsten call you the minute the interview is over. Okay?"

"Okay. Thanks." Thor hung up the phone and ran his hands over his face. He had it bad. Here he was, a man who'd started a company from scratch and built it into a multimillion-dollar business, yet he was afraid of a relationship with a woman. What was his problem? He stopped that thought before it took him places he didn't want to go.

He could still feel the hurt from the three serious relationships he'd had with women. Every time he'd been sure this one was right. Twice Erik had warned him to be careful; the third time Kirsten had been the one to caution him. He hadn't listened that time until almost too late.

Loki padded across the room and rested his chin on Thor's leg. Thor stroked the dog's silky cheek. "I've been ignoring you two, haven't I?" Odin rose from the rug and ambled over to get his share of attention. "After Kirsten calls I'll take you out for a walk. Maybe we'll hunt some rabbits."

At the mention of hunting, the dogs' ears perked up. Loki trotted to the door and whined, looking back to see what was taking Thor so long.

"I have to wait for one more call." Thor clenched his fist to keep from picking up the phone and dialing again.

His hand had just wrapped around the phone when it rang. "Larson."

"Larson, who?" At Kirsten's lilting laugh Odin tilted his head to one side. "I thought this was a grizzly bear answering my brother's phone."

"Sorry." Thor knew he'd been gruff. "I'm a little testy right now."

"Testy? Try badger with its foot caught in a trap. No, I think the badger would be easier to take."

"I'm not that bad," Thor growled. "So how did the interview go?"

"She's right here. You want to ask her?"

Thor's heart plummeted. "You didn't tell her. She's not. . ."

In the background he could hear Erik joining Kirsten in laughing. "That was a rotten dirty trick. I think I'm going to give both of you a pay cut just to bring you down to size."

"You can't do that, brother dear. We're indispensable." He could imagine Kirsten waving her hand in an airy gesture.

"The interview," Thor reminded her.

"Oh, that." Kirsten finally turned serious. "You're right, Thor. She's wonderful. I loved her ideas. We spent quite a bit of time discussing her job description, and once she warmed up she had some great input. In fact, she had me wondering how we've managed without someone like her all this time."

"When is she starting?" Thor couldn't keep the eagerness from his voice.

"She's thinking it over," Kirsten said. "I think she's holding out for more money."

Before Thor could respond in horror he heard Erik in the background. "That was the meanest thing you've said in a long time, Kirsten."

"Sorry, Thor. Erik's right." Kirsten sounded humbled. "I just wanted you to know she's different from the others. She was more interested in the work than in how much she would make. I had to bring up the salary." She paused. "Monday. She starts Monday."

Relief flooded Thor. He had no idea why he felt this way. Staying away from Jazmyn had become a priority, so why did he want to know her schedule? Why did he care?

When Thor hung up the phone Loki danced in place in front of the door. The dog was too smart for his own good. Shoving back from his desk, Thor stood and arched his back to stretch his muscles. "I think instead of going hunting, we'll do a little fishing." Both dogs stared at him as if they were hanging on every word. "I could use a little time to relax. Now that I've gotten Jazmyn settled with a good job, I don't have to worry about her."

He followed the dogs out the door, trying to convince himself that he wouldn't think about her anymore.

twelve

Settling back against the bank, Thor kept one hand on the fishing pole and an eye on the line leading down into the small lake. This was the life. Up early to catch a fish or two for breakfast. Several hours of business conducted in quiet from his place in the mountains. An afternoon hike ending with some more fishing, or hunting when it was in season, to get his supper.

What were the drawbacks? None. No power meetings filled with stress. No personnel problems to deal with. No women trying to cheat him out of everything he had worked for. No ties, except for a few with his family.

He could take on guide jobs if and when he wanted. This was what freedom was all about.

The dogs trotted out of the brush and flung themselves down on either side of him, panting from their run. Thor sighed. Even the dogs were contented.

Over a week had passed since Jazmyn went to work for T.L. Enterprises. Although he'd talked with Kirsten a few times to see how Jazmyn was doing, he'd managed to keep from going to town to check up on things. At that thought his stomach knotted. Staying away had taken every ounce of willpower he had. He didn't know how much longer he could do this.

A tug on his pole drew his attention. He reeled in the line, bringing up the smallest trout he'd ever caught. Loki cocked his head as if asking what his master had brought out of the lake. Thor chuckled.

"I think we'll give up on fishing for today." He unhooked the squirming fish and tossed it back into the water. "Let's go, boys."

Excitement coursed through him. He lengthened his stride, wanting to get home. The dogs trotted beside him, guarding him from every imagined threat in the forest. They were good dogs.

After washing his hands at the sink in back, he almost ran to the office. He didn't have any messages, so he clicked on the phone and speed-dialed Kirsten's number. She answered on the third ring.

"This is Kirsten." She sounded brusque. Thor frowned. She had to know it was he.

"Kirsten? This is Thor."

"Yes, sir. How can I help you?"

"Cut it out, Kirsty." Thor used the nickname he and Erik had taunted Kirsten with when they were kids. She always hated it. "I'm calling to see how things are going."

"Could you hold a minute, sir?" Thor could still hear her muffled voice talking. "Can we finish going over these layouts tomorrow, Jazmyn? This call is important, and it's almost time to go."

His heart raced as he listened to the woman in the background. Even if Kirsten hadn't said her name, he would have known Jazmyn's voice. He heard it in his dreams. Sometimes he even heard her as he walked through the forest.

Kirsten came back on the line. "Are you so thick-headed you can't get a hint? I should have just told Jazmyn this was my lunkhead of a brother who checks up on her every day."

"I haven't called that often."

"Yes, you have. You've called every day, although I have to admit this time is different."

"How's that?" Thor almost didn't want to hear her answer.

"This is the first day you've called before quitting time."

Thor picked up his watch. He'd left it on the desk when he went fishing. Time had seemed to fly by. He'd assumed it was later in the day. He hadn't checked the hour before calling.

"Sorry, Kirsten." He rubbed his hand over his face. "I didn't notice how early it was. I haven't called you every day."

"Oh, that's true." Kirsten gave a dramatic sigh. "You didn't call me on Sunday. You did call on Saturday, however, to get an overview of the week. Thor, I'm thinking of getting my phone number changed just so I don't get any more calls from you."

"I'm concerned about a new employee because hers is a new position, that's all."

"Yeah, right. You may be deluding yourself, Thor, but no one else is fooled."

"No one?" Panic made him sit up straight. "Whom have you talked to about this?"

"Don't have a cow." Kirsten laughed. "Only Erik and I know. Of course, I may have mentioned it to Wes. We don't keep secrets, you know."

"Okay, so tell me how she's working out."

"The same as yesterday." He could picture Kirsten rolling her eyes. "Some of the designs and layouts she's come up with are incredible. I think sales are increasing, too, but it's a little early to tell. You'll have to give her more than ten days of work to know for sure."

"Does she seem to be enjoying the job?"

"Yes."

"What is it?" Thor gripped the phone hard. "What's wrong?"

"Oh, it's probably nothing. I need to go. Wes is coming to take me out to dinner tonight. I have to freshen up before he gets here."

"Kirsten. What is it? I know something's wrong."

"Look, Thor, it's probably nothing. Jazmyn just looks a little tired. Haunted maybe. Perhaps she isn't getting enough sleep or something is keeping her awake."

"Does she act afraid?" Thor wondered if Jazmyn's fears had returned.

"No, not afraid. I don't know. I have the feeling she has something on her mind, but we don't know each other well enough for her to share. Maybe her brother will be back soon and she can talk to him."

"Is he out of town?"

"He's helping some friend of his take pictures for a book. He'll be gone for several weeks, I think." Kirsten groaned. "Look at the time. Thor, I have to go. I'll be home later, but don't call me. If there's anything to tell, I'll call you. Don't worry about Jazmyn. She'll be fine."

Clicking off the phone, Thor began to pace. Loki and Odin watched him from their spots along the wall. Restless energy seemed to make sitting down impossible.

What was upsetting Jazmyn? Had she met some guy in the office? T.L. Enterprises was a big company. They had a lot of employees, including many single men. Had one of them approached Jazmyn? She didn't trust men. Maybe she wanted to keep her job but was afraid of the bozo who was after her. Anger burned in his chest.

"We'll see about this." Thor strode to his bedroom, pulled out a bag, and began to throw a few essentials in it. With Jason out of town and something upsetting Jazmyn, he intended to see what he could do to help.

He made the trip in record time. As he drove up the long driveway, a car turned in behind him. He climbed out of his truck as Kirsten opened the door of her car.

"I can't believe this." She was laughing as she ran to hug him. "Ugh. You didn't even take the time to shower. You smell like fish."

"I'm thinking someone from work is after her. Do you have any idea who?"

Kirsten glanced at her husband, who was sauntering toward them. "Thor, I don't think anything is wrong with Jazmyn. At least not anything that wouldn't be cured by seeing you again."

❧

Jazmyn's footsteps echoed in the garage as she headed to the elevator that would take her to her office. She still couldn't believe she'd gotten this job. All these years she'd been afraid to go out and find something. Money wasn't an issue for her, so the income didn't matter. Her father had left a trust fund for her, and as long as she lived modestly, it would take care of her needs.

What she'd always wanted was to find a job that challenged her artistic skills. This position was perfect. She could incorporate her design ideas and the computer knowledge she had accumulated over the years.

At first Jazmyn was overwhelmed to be working so closely with a powerful woman like Kirsten Barnes. She'd expected her to be harsh and driven. Kirsten proved to be the opposite. Although she could get people to do the work, she was also funny and compassionate. Everyone in the company loved her.

In the elevator she leaned back against the wall and closed her eyes. Images of the mountains crossed her mind. She could almost hear the ripple of the river and see the chipmunks playing. How she missed being there.

She tried to push away thoughts of how much she missed seeing Thor. The rumble of his deep voice still came to her in her dreams. Sometimes she thought she saw him. This morning, on the way to work, she'd been sure he was following her in his truck. Then, two blocks from work, the truck turned off and sped away. It couldn't have been him.

"Lord, I want to see him so much I'm hallucinating." She

shook her head. "What am I supposed to do?"

The elevator dinged and opened. Jazmyn stepped off, heading to her office. She'd come in before regular hours on purpose. Kirsten told her yesterday she could set her own schedule if she had something else to do. Today she had plans for the afternoon.

She'd been working for an hour when Kirsten stuck her head in the doorway. "You sure got here early. Big plans this afternoon?"

"Yeah." Jazmyn tried to sound casual. "I thought I'd go hiking somewhere."

"It's still pretty hot. Do you do much hiking?"

Jazmyn shrugged. "No. A few weeks ago I found out how out of shape I am. I thought I'd try to do something about it."

"Gotcha. You might try going to a gym. I can give you the name of the one I go to. It's not far from here. They'll give you advice on what exercises to do so you don't do too much at first. It can be fun."

"That might be a good idea." Jazmyn smiled. "That's probably smarter than going off hiking."

"Okay, I'll call you with the name and number. If you decide to join, we can work out together sometimes."

"That sounds good." Warmth flooded Jazmyn. She'd never been allowed to have girlfriends growing up.

"By the way, what are you doing for lunch today?" Kirsten asked.

"Probably the deli down the street." Jazmyn made a face. "I think I'm stuck on deli food."

Kirsten laughed. "See you later. I'd better earn my keep."

The morning raced by. When Jazmyn checked her watch she was startled to find that lunchtime was almost past. Grabbing her purse, she headed for the door.

Heat blasted her as she stepped outside. A light breeze

ruffled her hair. Traffic noise and exhaust fumes made her long for the mountains once more. Maybe when Jason returned they could go back for a weekend.

The deli wasn't far. Most of the people were already leaving, their lunch hours almost up. Pushing open the door, Jazmyn breathed in the scent of fresh-baked bread. This place was the best find since coming to work down here. She loved the food.

The bell at the door jingled as she stepped up to the counter to order, and the person who entered got into line behind her. A frazzled clerk waited for her order.

"You know," Jazmyn said, craning her neck to see into the display case next to her, "I have this terrible craving for something chocolate. I think I'll have one of those brownies, too."

"Be careful. Some squirrel might steal it."

Jazmyn whirled around, her hand going to her throat. Thor. It was he. She wasn't imagining this time. He looked so good he took her breath away. "What are you doing here?"

He shrugged. "It's a public place, isn't it?"

Her face warmed. "You know what I mean. In town. I thought you hated the city."

"I do come into civilization every few months for supplies. Mind if I sit with you?" He leaned past her and gave the clerk his order. Jazmyn tried to still her pounding heart. How would she ever carry her food to the table when her hands were shaking so badly?

Niggling reminders that Thor wasn't a Christian pushed at the back of her mind. She ignored them. She wasn't pursuing a romantic interest but visiting with a friend she hadn't seen in a while. This couldn't be the same as the unequal yoking Jason talked about.

Thor stood so close they were almost touching. Jazmyn had to force herself not to lean against him. She couldn't help thinking about the way he'd held her the night she got lost. A shiver ran through her.

"Where would you like to sit?" His question startled her. He held a tray with both their food and drinks. "Lead the way."

She didn't realize until she reached the table that she'd picked one in a corner away from the other diners. She slipped into a chair. Thor sat across from her. His hand brushed hers as he handed her the sandwich she'd ordered. The contact was electric. Her eyes met his. He smiled, his gaze warm and enticing.

"So, how's the new job?"

She looked up. "How did you know?"

"I saw you coming out of the building." He shrugged. "I just put two and two together."

"It's fine." She unwrapped her sandwich and bit off a small piece. She didn't know if she'd be able to eat with Thor there. His presence did strange things to her. How had he known where she'd be? Did he ask one of the men he knew at T.L. Enterprises about her? She was pretty sure he didn't just happen to run into her.

thirteen

"So, are you going to share that brownie with me, or do I have to be like Xena and fight for a bite?" Thor was already reaching for the huge brownie. Jazmyn wanted to shake her head to make sure she wasn't dreaming he was there.

"They have more brownies. You can buy your own." She tried for a saucy tone, rather than sounding as breathless as she felt.

"My mother always said you have to finish your meal before you can have dessert." Thor grinned. "You've stopped eating and still have half a sandwich left. That means I should get the whole brownie because I finished my meal."

"Then you're probably too full to eat any sweets. Those sandwiches are big enough to fill an elephant." Jazmyn reached for the brownie. Before she could pluck it up from the napkin where she'd placed it, Thor covered her hand with his. Her mouth went dry.

He leaned closer across the small table. "I think we should share this."

"On one condition." They were almost nose-to-nose. Jazmyn could smell the woodsy scent of his cologne.

"What condition is that?"

"I. . .um. I'm getting off early this afternoon. If you're not doing anything else, why don't you run some errands with me?" She couldn't believe she'd said that. Never in her life had she asked a man to do something with her. Her cheeks felt like they were on fire.

"Deal." Thor lifted her hand and retrieved the brownie.

"See, I'll do anything for chocolate."

"And you accused Xena of being that way because she's a female." Jazmyn took her half and bit into the delicious sweet. "If I didn't know better, I'd accuse you of being a chauvinist." She winked at him and almost choked on her bite. Never in her life had she flirted with a man like this. Not even Adam. Theirs had been a steady, safe relationship. Around Thor her emotions seemed to be on a roller coaster.

The afternoon dragged by. Thor had agreed to meet her outside the building at three o'clock. She couldn't seem to concentrate on her work.

Maddy knocked and stuck her head through the door. "Jazmyn?"

"Come on in." Jazmyn smiled at the perky redhead. In the past week and a half, she had gotten to know Maddy pretty well.

"Kirsten had to leave early. She asked me to get these papers to you. This is a list of new products we're thinking of adding to our line. She wanted you to work up some display ideas and get them to her as soon as possible."

"Does she need this done today?"

"Nah." Maddy rested her hip against the side of the desk, a sure sign she planned to stay a few minutes. "Tomorrow, or even the next day, will be fine. You know what they say. No rest for the wicked."

Jazmyn lifted her eyebrow. "And you think I'm wicked?"

"I'm not answering that one. So, have you read the memo about the party?"

"Party?" Jazmyn frowned. "I didn't get any memo like that. Is someone retiring?"

"No. This is the big bash the boss puts on every year. The salaried personnel get invited to his mansion, where we stuff ourselves with food we could never afford. He usually has some sort of band or something to entertain everyone. There's a pool if you want to swim. It's great."

"Well, I must not be invited, because I haven't heard anything about it." Jazmyn felt relieved. Attending an event like that would only make her nervous. If they didn't invite her, she wouldn't feel obligated to go. "Maybe I'm too new to be included."

"I doubt that." Maddy crossed her arms. "I always go on the off chance I might get a glimpse of the mysterious big boss."

"Mysterious?"

"Yeah, the guy who started the company. He's some sort of a recluse. Doesn't like people."

"So how did he start a company that's so successful? I'd think you'd need to be a people person for that."

"Oh, no. He has others do that part for him. That's where Kirsten and her brother, Erik, come in. Rumor has it they're related to the big boss, but I don't know for sure. I haven't been here that long."

"It always amazes me how the rumor mill works everywhere you go," Jazmyn said. "I don't care what the man is like as long as I'm allowed to do my job."

"You will come, though, won't you?" Maddy began to rummage through Jazmyn's in-box. "I know you've got an invitation here somewhere. Aha!" She pulled out a white folded paper.

Jazmyn took the memo and read it. Tension tightened her muscles. She didn't want to have to attend some fancy party at a mansion. She wasn't interested in some mysterious boss. "I don't know that I'll be able to make it. This sounds pretty formal. I don't have anything to wear."

"You have four weeks to shop," Maddy countered. "If I have to, I'll take you to find something. You're going if I have to drag you there. It will be fun. Besides, how often do you get to go inside some swanky place? You won't believe how amazing this house is."

"You're impossible, Maddy." Jazmyn laughed. "Maybe Kirsten is right, and you're really mad after all."

"I'll be mad if you don't go with me." She wrinkled her nose at Jazmyn before she closed the door on her way out.

Jazmyn sighed and stared at the paper in her hand. She only wanted a job she enjoyed. She didn't want to see a fancy house or a reclusive boss. Four weeks. That gave her plenty of time to come up with an excuse. Maybe by then Jason would be back and they could make some plans. Right now she had to finish a few things and get ready to meet Thor. Her pulse sped up at the thought.

❧

Standing across the street from the T.L. Enterprises office building, Thor tried to act casual. Inside he burned with impatience. Having lunch with Jazmyn only whetted his appetite for spending more time with her. Now that he was in town he didn't want to let her out of his sight. He tried to assure himself he was only checking up on a new employee's job satisfaction, but inside he knew better.

He still couldn't bring himself to tell Jazmyn he owned this company. Since he hadn't spent much time in the offices during the last few years, he didn't worry about anyone identifying him. Most of the employees were new enough that they didn't know Thor. Even Erik wasn't as visible as Kirsten. He supposed most of the workers thought Erik was the elusive boss.

The door across the street swung open. Jazmyn stepped out into the heat, fumbling with a pair of sunglasses to guard against the glaring sun. She didn't dress like a lot of businesswomen in power suits with padded shoulders. She wore an airy sort of dress with a floral print and a skirt that twirled in the light breeze. Her hair lay loose about her shoulders. Even from here Thor could see the highlights glinting in the sun.

He pushed off from the wall and strode across the street. The moment Jazmyn noticed him she lit up with a smile that brightened the day. His stomach did a flip-flop. Thor stuck his hands in his pockets to keep from pulling her into his arms and kissing her.

"Ready to go?" She tilted her head back to look up at him. He loved the fact that she didn't step away. When they first met she'd been terrified of him.

"I have to tell you, I'm not much of a shopper." He breathed deep, loving the fresh-washed scent of her.

"Neither is Jason. He doesn't seem to understand that when I go looking for a blouse to go with a skirt, the blouse not only has to be the right color, but the right style and material, too. Jason just wants to grab the first blouse he sees and leave the store."

"I knew I liked him for some reason." Thor grinned. "We shop the same way. Of course, buying flannel shirts to match my jeans isn't quite as difficult."

She laughed. He loved the sound of it and wanted to make her laugh some more.

"So which way are we headed? My truck is parked around the corner."

She hesitated. "My first stop is a little embarrassing, but I made the appointment this morning before I knew you'd be coming along."

"We can meet later if this is a problem." Thor tried to cover his disappointment.

"No. I. . .um, my boss, Kirsten, gave me the name of the gym where she works out. I have an appointment with a trainer there. She's going to show me around and talk about an exercise program for me."

He frowned. "I hope you're not doing this because you

think you're fat. Women are always thinking they have to lose weight."

"I'm doing it because I couldn't walk ten feet up a mountain without having to stop and catch my breath. I want to get in better shape." She paused and glanced around. "You know, in case Jason and I go up to the mountains again."

A thrill shot through Thor. She liked the outdoors. He wasn't sure she'd ever want to go camping again, but she liked it. He thought he could float on air about now.

At the gym Thor waited in the lobby as Jazmyn followed a female bodybuilder into the inner sanctum. He waved them on, knowing he didn't want to chance going inside. This was the place where both Kirsten and Erik worked out. He might run into someone who had seen him with them before, and he didn't want to take the risk.

"Bored to pieces?" Jazmyn asked as she breezed into the lobby a half-hour later.

Thor tossed down the magazine he'd been leafing through and stood up. "Not a bit. Just gathering my strength for this marathon of shopping." As he pushed open the door for her, he put his hand on her back. He couldn't seem to resist touching her.

"I need to run by the mall."

"What, more exercise already? Your shoes don't look the type for running in."

"We'll take your truck, smarty. Bridget, my trainer, suggested getting my workout clothes at a store there. She says I can flash my membership card and get a discount." She gave him a wide smile as he opened the truck door for her. "I love discounts."

"The mall it is." Thor climbed into the truck, trying to hide his dismay. How had he gotten into this mess? He hated shopping, and most of all he hated malls. He made it a point never to go into one unless someone dragged him kicking and screaming. What was it about Jazmyn that had him eager to follow her anywhere? The thought of her in the mountains, out of her element, flashed through his mind. If she could do that, he could brave the mall.

School was out for the day, so the mall was teeming with teenagers.

"I haven't come here in a long time." Jazmyn leaned close to be heard above the din. She looked a little nervous.

Thor leaned down and spoke into her ear as he put his arm around her. "I remember when you were afraid of everything. You've changed so much I can't believe it."

A smile lit her eyes, those beautiful green eyes a man could get lost in. "Jason has been such a help, but I have to say all the credit goes to God and the peace He's given me. I have verses of Scripture memorized to battle my fears. At first I didn't think that would work, but I'm amazed at the courage God's given me."

Several times in the last few weeks Thor had found himself pondering the faith Jazmyn and Jason shared. They reminded him so much of his mother. He'd always thought only weak people needed God, but maybe this wasn't all about weakness and strength but something else entirely. When Jason got back, he wanted to find a time to talk to him about his faith.

"Here we are." Jazmyn led him into a store. The noise level dropped several decibels. Thor sighed with relief.

"I'll need shoes and some workout clothes." Jazmyn's mouth twisted as she perused the various racks and displays in the store.

"Here's what you need." He led her down an aisle to a rack of stretchy workout clothes. He started to pluck off a green set that would match her eyes, but the hanger caught on the rod.

He had pulled too hard. The display tipped. Thor grabbed

for the rod and missed. The resulting crash brought store personnel running. He still held the green outfit, while the rest lay in a heap of color at his feet.

"This one would look good on you." He offered the outfit to Jazmyn as she covered her mouth to stifle the laughter.

fourteen

"I think you owe me big time. That was a nightmare."

"Which part?" Jazmyn was obviously trying hard not to laugh again. Inside the store she'd laughed until she had tears in her eyes. He wouldn't tell her this, but he'd loved the sound of her laughter.

"What do you mean, which part?"

"Well, there was the part where you knocked over the exercise outfits. That, at least, was colorful."

"Go ahead. Laugh." He bit the inside of his lip to keep from joining her. It had been funny.

"Then there was the display of shoes you bumped into."

"They shouldn't have left all those boxes out in the middle where anyone could run into them." Thor could still see all the boxes skittering across the floor in every direction. He could also recall the look of horror on the faces of the staff.

"My personal favorite had to be when you got bored waiting for me and decided to try out the fishing equipment. I doubt if anyone had ever hooked, and tried to reel in, a security camera before." Tears shone in her eyes.

Thor laughed. "Okay, that's enough. Since you think I'm so amusing, I'm insisting you have dinner with me. After all this trauma, I can't face the thought of eating alone."

Jazmyn took a deep breath and wiped her eyes. "I don't know. I'm not sure if there's any safe food out there. I didn't bring bibs with me." They both laughed again.

Carrying her bags in one hand, Thor reached over and pulled Jazmyn close. Her green eyes sparkled as she looked up at him. Thor realized he'd stopped in the middle of the mall parking lot. His pulse raced. He wanted nothing more than to kiss this woman.

Lifting their two hands together, he traced his thumb along her lower lip. Her lips parted. He could see a smattering of freckles dusted across her nose. He leaned closer.

A car horn honked, spoiling the moment. They stepped to one side to let a teenager drive past, his stereo booming loud enough to shake the ground.

Somehow Thor had ended up with his arm around Jazmyn, holding her snug against his side. He loosened his hold. "So, I know this little Italian place. They give out big bibs for messy eaters."

The tension of the moment faded. "That sounds like a plan," Jazmyn said.

As Thor headed them toward his truck, he ignored the warning lights flashing inside his head. The promise he'd made never to get involved with another woman seemed so distant now. He couldn't recall ever feeling this way before. Had he ever laughed like this with one of his fiancées? He didn't think so. Those relationships had all been about status and show.

Bruno's Restaurant was a quaint mix of Italian and Southwest. When they walked in, the hostess led them to a quiet table in the corner. The table was small enough so that their knees touched when they sat down. Thor tried to ignore how much he enjoyed this contact with Jazmyn.

He watched her from the corner of his eye. She was trying to decide what to order and couldn't seem to make up her mind. Perhaps she didn't like Italian food.

"I'm sorry, I didn't ask if you like Italian food," Thor said.

She smiled as she looked up. "This is my favorite kind of food. I haven't eaten out much, though. I didn't realize how expensive a place like this could be."

He hadn't expected her to be concerned over prices. He'd never been out with a woman who worried about how much he spent on her. In fact, he usually couldn't splurge enough.

"Order what you like. I wouldn't have brought you here if I couldn't afford it."

"I'm sorry. I didn't mean to imply anything." Jazmyn laid her menu down and smoothed the pages. "What are you ordering?"

"This place has the best ravioli I've ever eaten. They make it right here, even the sauce. It's an old family recipe. I knew the owners years ago. Anyway, I always order the ravioli, but everything's good. What's your favorite?"

Her gaze dropped to the menu. "Well, my absolute favorite has to be eggplant parmigiana."

"Then that's what you should have." Thor lifted his hand, motioning to the waitress that they were ready to order.

They sat for a long time talking after their meal. She was the first woman who seemed to enjoy hearing his stories of guiding hunters into the mountains. He couldn't remember the last time he'd talked so much about himself. Every time he tried to change the conversation to something about her, Jazmyn avoided his question and asked one of her own.

Only a few stars were out as Thor walked Jazmyn to the garage under the T.L. Enterprises building. How he wished this was the forest where stars were plentiful and the air was pure, not filled with exhaust fumes.

"Thank you for dinner." Jazmyn fished her keys from her purse, clicking the button to unlock her car. She smiled up at him. "Thanks, too, for the entertainment earlier."

"I aim to please. That's my motto," Thor said. He reached around her to open the car door. Before she could turn away, he cupped her cheek and drew her close. Her eyes drifted shut. The kiss he gave her was warm and sweet, full of promise. "Thanks for seeing me today." He stepped back, opening the door wide. "When you talk to him, tell Jason I'd like to see him when he gets back to town."

"I will." Her eyes glittered in the dim light. Was she crying? Thor frowned and started toward her, but she pulled the door shut. He watched as she left the garage. Had he done something to upset her?

❧

For a long time Jazmyn lay awake thinking about the fun she'd had with Thor. She could still feel the sweetness of his kiss on her lips. Every time she thought about the mall and his clumsiness there, she had to laugh. Who would have thought? In the woods he seemed to be able to do anything, but in civilization he was out of his element.

Even so, Thor had tried hard to enjoy the places she wanted to go. The only time all evening that he'd been anything other than considerate was when she told him about the party T.L. Enterprises was having for the employees. When she mentioned the elusive owner and the rumors about him, Thor's eyes darkened. She changed the subject, not knowing what had upset him. Could it be he was jealous? That would be crazy, because she didn't care at all about the man who owned her company.

The alarm seemed to ring almost before she got to sleep. Her eyes were gritty. A morning shower and coffee revived her somewhat, but she wanted to go back to bed and sleep for another day at least. For what seemed the millionth time she wished Jason were home. She needed someone to talk to about her attraction to Thor. She didn't want it to become anything serious, yet she did enjoy his company.

"Morning, girl." Maddy smiled at Jazmyn as she dragged off the elevator. "You look like you had some night."

"Couldn't sleep." Jazmyn stifled a yawn. "If you hold my

work, I could kick back in my office and catch some z's."

"I don't think that's going to happen. I've heard the big boss is in town, and he wants to see the designs for the new products. Maybe you'll get to meet him today when you're at your shiny best."

Jazmyn groaned. "That's all I need. Maybe I'll hide in the closet. You convince Kirsten I've been kidnapped and will only be released when the owner is gone again."

"I'll bring you a cup of my super-strength coffee. It's guaranteed to wake the dead."

"That sounds perfect." Jazmyn headed into her office.

Kirsten called to ask her if the new layouts were done. She didn't say anything about meeting with the boss, which filled Jazmyn with relief. Today was not the day for something like that.

"You're looking perkier." Maddy grinned at her from the open door. "Must be because it's almost quitting time."

"That's the best news I've had all day." Jazmyn brushed her hair back from her forehead. Maddy leaned against the doorframe and stared at her.

"Well, are you going to tell me or not?"

"Tell you what?"

"About your hot date last night." Maddy rolled her eyes. "The one that kept you up so late you almost didn't make it to work this morning."

"I wasn't even close to being late." Maddy was like a bulldog. Once she got ahold of an idea, she wouldn't let go until she worried it to death. "I did spend some time with a friend, but I didn't get home late."

"A friend?" Maddy's eyebrows rose. "As in a male sort of friend?"

"Yes." Jazmyn sighed. "He's only a friend, though. He knows my brother. It's nothing."

"Hmmm. I'll let you off this time. By the way, do you have a dress for the party yet?"

"I don't know if I'll go to the party, Maddy. It's not my thing."

"You're going." Maddy studied her. "I thought this weekend we could get together and shop for your dress. I think you need something that will knock the socks off all those eligible bachelors."

"Maddy, I'm not in the market for a husband. I don't want to knock their socks off. Then you have all those smelly bare feet."

Maddy laughed. "Girlfriend, we have to get you to that party. You don't know what you're missing. Tell you what. I heard they're having a sale at that little boutique in the mall, Lacy's. Why don't we run over there after work and just look around?" She gave Jazmyn a woeful look that made Jazmyn laugh.

"Okay. Let me finish up here, and I'll be ready to go. Maybe we can try out that new coffee shop and deli while we're there. I heard some of the girls talking about it the other day, saying it's really good."

"As long as you don't make me eat bean sprouts or something like that." Maddy patted her ample hips. "I have to keep up my image."

Jazmyn giggled and shook her head as Maddy closed the door. She'd never dreamed how much fun having a friend could be. She thought of last night when she and Thor had been together. She'd enjoyed the time they spent talking and laughing. Growing up, she'd missed out on friendships like those. Now she treasured the few she had.

The mall was teeming with people. Jazmyn stuck close to Maddy as they wended their way through the throngs.

"Here we go." Maddy looped her arm through Jazmyn's and slipped past a couple of women coming out of Lacy's laden with shopping bags. "I was in here last week. They have some really cute dresses back here."

Jazmyn followed Maddy through the maze of racks. She couldn't help but smile as she recalled Thor in the sports store last night. He would be a terror here where the clothes were so close together you had to squeeze to get past.

Maddy yanked a bright red dress from a rack and held it up to Jazmyn.

"I can't possibly wear this." Jazmyn took the hanger and put the wisp of cloth back.

"Why not? It's perfect."

"First of all, it's indecent. A front like that would show off my belly button." She chuckled at Maddy's look of outrage. "Well, maybe it wasn't that revealing, but it was too low-cut for me. Second, I don't like wearing red. It's too bright."

"It would be perfect with your hair and eyes though." Maddy, not to be defeated, started rummaging through the clothes again.

A flash of green caught Jazmyn's eye. The color of the outfit Thor held up for her last night. The one he said would look perfect with her coloring. She reached for the dress. It was simple and beautiful. Deep down she knew it was fruitless to pick an outfit because of Thor. He wouldn't even be at the party.

She held the dress in front of her. "What about this one?"

Maddy turned. Her eyes widened. "You'll not only knock their socks off, they'll drop their teeth."

"Oh, great." Jazmyn grimaced. "Now I have a bunch of toothless guys with smelly feet."

fifteen

Pacing the floor, Thor felt like a tiger trapped in a cage. He'd been in town three days and already he was going nuts. Only the hope of seeing Jazmyn again kept him here.

"Sit down before you wear a hole in the carpet." Kirsten took a sip of her tea and leaned back in the plush chair. She had been going over some reports for the company. "Your pacing won't get Erik here any faster."

"Where is he?" Thor stopped near the window, gazing at the empty driveway. "Did you check to see if his plane came in late?"

"Thor, he only landed forty-five minutes ago. It takes that long to drive here from the airport. Plus, he still had to get his luggage and meet the driver. Be patient." She smiled. "Oh, I forgot who I'm talking to."

"I am patient," Thor growled, then realized how he sounded. "At least I'm patient with some things. Right now I'm having a little trouble." He sighed. "Is she—?"

"Yes, Thor, Jazmyn is working out just fine. How many times do I have to tell you this? She and Maddy have hit it off. Yesterday they even went shopping, as you know, since you were watching from the building across the street. Don't you feel guilty spying on the woman?"

"I wasn't spying." Thor shoved his hands in the pockets of his jeans. "I thought maybe I'd run into her again. I worry about her getting lonely with her brother out of town. She doesn't have any friends, you know."

"Well, that's changing. She has Maddy, and she has me."

Kirsten flashed him a smile. "Since she joined my gym the other day, we made plans to work out together a couple times a week."

Panic raced through Thor. "You can't do that."

"Why not? I like her."

"What if you let something slip? I don't want her to know yet."

"Thor, she's not at all like Dana or Melissa or. . .what was the other one? Gloria." Kirsten sighed. "I know they hurt you, but you can't judge the world by greedy women like them. You were a different person then, too."

"I haven't changed." He moved closer to the window, putting his back to Kirsten.

"If I remember right, back then you were enamored with wealth and power, Bro. Now you aren't. That makes you a different person to me." Kirsten's soft words struck deep in Thor. She was right. For a long time, when his company first became profitable in a big way, he'd been riding high on the excitement of fame and fortune. It had taken three times of being duped for him to come crashing back to reality.

"I still can't trust her. I have to be sure she isn't like them." His eyes stung. Yes, he'd been hurt, but that had been because of his own stupidity. He would not allow that to happen again. Ever.

Thoughts of his time spent with Jason popped into his mind. On one of their long walks Thor had mentioned his distrust of women. Jason had talked to Thor about Jesus. He said that Jesus had been betrayed by everyone He called a friend. They'd all run off and left Him to die. Even so, Jesus asked God to forgive all the wrongs done to Him.

Forgive. His mother had always talked about forgiving and not judging others by what one person had done. But three? He'd had three women do the same thing to him. Could it be that part of it was his fault? Was Kirsten right? If he hadn't been so greedy and power-hungry, would he have seen the shallowness of those women earlier?

A glint of light caught his eye. The long, dark car pulling into the drive would be Erik returning from his trip. He'd been out of the country doing business for the company. Erik was the liaison, making deals elsewhere for them, while Kirsten handled the local needs of the business. Few people in the company building where Kirsten worked had even met Erik. That's why Thor hoped his plan would work.

For the next thirty minutes chaos reigned as Erik's luggage was brought in and he changed into more comfortable clothes. Several of the hired help wanted to come by and greet him after his absence. Thor continued to pace the floor, waiting for his turn.

"So, Bro, what brings you in from the wilds?" Erik sank onto the sofa, plunking his long legs on an ottoman.

"A woman," Kirsten said.

"What?" Erik's eyebrows shot up. "I thought you'd sworn off."

"It's not what you think." Thor glared at Kirsten, who crossed her eyes at him. "I came into town to ask you a favor and to check up on an employee."

"Would this employee happen to be female?" Erik's smug look made Thor want to start growling again. "Would her name happen to be Jazmyn? I haven't met her yet, but I can see that will have to change."

"She's a friend only. I'm concerned about her."

"I see." Erik nodded and put his hands behind his head. "So what's the favor you need? If it's anything more strenuous than rest and relaxation for today, I don't know if I'll comply."

"It's about the party next Saturday. I want you to pretend to be me."

Erik laughed. "Haven't I been doing that for years?" Thor

hadn't been a visible part of the business in a long time.

"I want you to go a step further. I want you to meet her as if you're me."

"Thor, if you're planning what I think you're planning, this isn't a good idea." Kirsten frowned at him. "This could backfire on you."

Heaviness settled in Thor's chest. He knew the risk he was taking. Erik was the charming one. He had a charisma that attracted women to him, although he'd never returned the feeling with any one woman. What if Jazmyn fell for him? What if she became enamored with the status Erik represented? His shoulders slumped.

"I have to know, Kirsten. If she's like them, I want to know before this goes any further."

"What's going on?" Erik's brows drew together as he looked from Kirsten to Thor.

"Your brother is in love with this woman." Kirsten smirked as Thor started to protest. "I'm guessing he wants you to give her a test and see if she passes before he pursues the relationship. Am I right?"

"You don't understand, Kirsten. You're happy with Wes. You got a good man the first time." Thor turned to look back out the window before emotion clouded his speech.

A moment later Kirsten came up and hugged him. "Jazmyn is a wonderful person, Thor. You've changed. I think she'll be perfect for you."

ও

Stepping from the car, Jazmyn willed her knees not to shake as she stared up at the imposing house. She smoothed her dress, wishing she could return home and curl up in her bed with a good book. This was the last place in the world she wanted to be.

"Impressive, isn't it?" Maddy said. They'd ridden together in

Maddy's car. Jazmyn had hesitated, knowing she would be dependent on Maddy to get home, but she knew she had to have someone go with her or she'd chicken out.

"If we leave right now, I'll take you someplace and buy you dinner, Maddy. We can talk girl-talk until all hours. Just please don't make me go in there." Jazmyn couldn't take her eyes from the well-lighted windows.

"No way, girlfriend. You've never seen a place like this one." Maddy looped her arm through Jazmyn's, dragging her toward the front door. "Come on. We're fashionably late. Let's get in there and see what's happening."

Jazmyn clenched her hands together, trying to get some warmth into her fingers. "I don't think I can do this." Her voice trembled.

"What have you been telling me ever since you started working at T.L.? Does that God of yours only give you courage at certain times and not others?"

Maddy was right. Jazmyn closed her eyes, praying for courage, for the fear to be taken from her. She was a child of God. There wasn't anything she couldn't do. She opened her eyes and took a deep breath. "Let's go."

"Maddy, Jazmyn. Welcome." Kirsten greeted them as the maid led them through the foyer. "Maddy, you know my brother, Erik. Jazmyn, this is Erik. Erik, Jazmyn."

The man standing beside Kirsten held out his hand to Maddy first. When he turned to Jazmyn he gave her a wink and folded her cold fingers inside his warm ones. Her hand seemed to disappear inside his. A picture of Thor and his huge frame flashed through Jazmyn's mind. For some reason Erik reminded her of him.

"Go on in and make yourselves at home. There's enough food and punch for an army." Kirsten waved her hand toward the groups of people gathered in the huge living room. "We'll join you as soon as the others have arrived."

Erik still held Jazmyn's hand. His eyes, a light, warm brown, gazed into hers. She tugged and he released her hand, giving her another wink as she turned away to follow Maddy.

Maddy leaned close as they moved away from Kirsten and Erik. "Well, girlfriend, you sure made an impression."

"Is that the elusive boss you spoke of?"

"Some people say so because he isn't around very much, but I've heard rumors that even Erik isn't the big guy. I don't think he started T.L."

"Will the founder be here tonight?" Jazmyn gazed around the room. She saw a few of the people she'd met in the last few weeks. Most of them, though, she'd never seen before because they worked in different departments from hers.

"He's never been here before. For all I know, Erik could be the founder. The other is just a rumor." Maddy grabbed her by the arm. "Come on. I see some people you have to meet."

Time passed in a swirl of faces and names that Jazmyn couldn't hope to remember later. She didn't know how Maddy knew so many people. The woman bubbled as she worked her way around the room, dragging Jazmyn behind her.

When they reached the doors that opened onto a lighted patio, Jazmyn excused herself and stepped outside. She had to get some fresh air, some quiet. A band had begun playing inside, and that, combined with the buzz of conversation, made Jazmyn want to get away.

A light breeze ruffled the loose strands of hair on her neck and around her face. The grass and trees around the house reminded her of the mountains. She could almost hear the rippling sound of the river that went past their camp.

"I see someone else needed to escape."

She swung around, startled to see Erik standing a few feet behind her. She hadn't heard him come outside.

"I'm sorry. Maybe I shouldn't be out here."

"No, you're fine. I wanted some fresh air, too. Kirsten is the people person. I do this once a year. The rest of the time she's the one who interacts with the employees."

"I see." Jazmyn wanted to go back inside, but she didn't want to be rude. She didn't feel comfortable with this stranger, even if he was Kirsten's brother.

"I hear you're our newest employee. Working in layout and design on computers. Am I right?" He gave her a warm smile.

She nodded. "I've only been with T.L. a few weeks. I guess that's why I've never met you at the office."

"Oh, I'm not there much. In fact, I just returned this past week from a business trip overseas. That's the part of the company Kirsten wants no part of. She wants to be home for Wes, and she hates to fly. Do you like the outdoors?" He gestured at the expansive grounds. A path wandered through them lighted by old-fashioned lampposts.

"I went to the mountains recently with my brother and a friend. Until then, I hadn't known how much I liked being outdoors. The smell is so fresh and clean." Jazmyn clamped her mouth shut, wishing she hadn't said so much.

Erik stepped forward and offered her his arm. "Take a walk with me." He smiled as she glanced back at the house. "Don't worry. They won't miss the two of us. We won't be long."

They strolled through the grounds. Erik stopped from time to time to point out a particular plant or tree to her. He talked about his trip overseas and his work with the company. Jazmyn began to relax. Something about Erik warmed her. She liked the man, mostly because he reminded her of someone else.

When they arrived back at the patio, Erik patted her hand before she let go of his arm. "I seem to have spent the whole time talking about myself. Typical male, I suppose." They both laughed.

He leaned close to her. "Would you like to go to dinner sometime? Then you could tell me all about you. I can afford to take you anyplace you want, you know."

She stepped back. "Thank you for the offer, Erik." Jazmyn looked out at the lawn. "I. . .um. There's someone." She hesitated. "I just can't." She fled through the doors into the bright, noisy room without looking back.

sixteen

The door clicked shut behind Jazmyn as she slipped into Maddy's office. She leaned against the wall, her heart pounding.

"What are you doing, girl?" Maddy stared at her from across the room. "Is the bogeyman after you?"

"Shhh." Jazmyn held her finger to her lips. A low murmur of voices came through the door then faded.

"You want to tell me what this is all about?" Maddy said.

"I didn't want him to see me."

"Who? Is one of those low-lifes bothering you?"

"It's. . .it's Erik. Kirsten's brother. He's been around a lot since the party. He keeps asking me to go out with him."

Maddy's mouth fell open. "You mean the hunk? You're hiding from him?" She shook her head. "Girl, I'd better call 911 and get you some help. That man could have his choice of a hundred girls just by snapping his fingers." She let out a low whistle.

"Then let him have those hundred girls. I don't want to be one of them." Jazmyn crossed to a chair and slumped down into it. "I didn't tell you about the night of the party and how he asked me out. He even hinted that he had enough money should I want to go out with him. As if money makes the difference."

"Well, to some of us it would." Maddy's eyes turned dreamy. "When you think about that incredible build and handsome face, I'd say money just adds the final touch to the picture." She gave an exaggerated sigh.

Jazmyn laughed. "Maddy, you're impossible. What happened

to the doctor you were talking about last week?"

"I found out the hours he works. And I found out about the cute little nurse who helps him more than she should."

"Yeah, well, I don't want to go out with anyone right now." Jazmyn pushed up from the chair. "I guess I'd better see if the coast is clear and get back to my office. It's time to go home, anyway, since I came in early." She grinned at Maddy. "Next time, I'll tell Erik to ask you."

"Girlfriend, you're the best." Maddy fanned her face. "You know, if I didn't think Kirsten would kill me, I'd apply to be Erik's personal secretary and fly all over the world with him. What a tough job."

Jazmyn smiled all the way to her office. Having a friend was wonderful. Maddy gave her plenty of opportunity to witness, and Jazmyn believed one of these days her new friend would become a Christian, too.

At home she kicked off her shoes and sank onto the couch with a sigh of relief. The last two weeks of work had been more stressful than before. Erik's pursuit had been subtle, but there. Although she found him attractive and nice, she had no romantic interest in him at all. He seemed to think she should.

She didn't want to admit that for some reason Erik reminded her of Thor. When he came around she couldn't keep her mind on her work, not because of an attraction to Erik, but because of his similarity to a backwoods guide. *Girl, you've got it bad.* She could hear Maddy's voice echoing in her head.

The phone trilled. She leaped up, hoping Jason had made it home. He'd called a few days ago to say he'd be in sometime today but probably late.

"Hello?"

"Jazmyn." Her heart lurched at the sound of Thor's low voice over the phone. "I called to see if Jason had gotten home."

Her heart plummeted. *That's okay,* she told herself, *you don't want to be around him, anyway. Remember the unequally yoked thing.*

"He's supposed to be home sometime today. I haven't heard from him though."

"Okay. I'll call him tomorrow." He paused. "I'm in town for a few days again."

"We could meet for lunch tomorrow." Here she was asking him out again! What was the matter with her?

"That would be great. Is one o'clock okay?"

"That's fine. I'll go in early and get the rest of the afternoon off." Jazmyn's hands were shaking as she hung up the phone. What had she been thinking? One minute she was determined not to have anything to do with the guy, and the next she was asking him to go out with her.

Mid-morning the next day, Jazmyn called the deli down the street. They had a special deal on picnic lunches they packed in boxes. Thor might appreciate going somewhere out of the way for a lunch instead of eating inside with a lot of other people. There was a park not far from here that might do. She'd worn slacks to work for this reason.

"Mornin', Jazmyn." She started as Erik came up behind her.

"Good morning." She stepped away from him. Erik always seemed to come right up beside her.

"How about going to lunch with me today?" Erik placed one of his big hands on the wall behind Jazmyn.

She sidled away. "I'm sorry, I already have plans."

"Too bad." He smiled, his handsome face close to hers. "When are you going to stop avoiding me and agree to go somewhere together? I know you're interested in someone else, but he can't give you what I can, can he?"

Jazmyn bristled with anger. "I don't find a man attractive for the size of his wallet. Now please leave me alone." She stalked down the hallway to her office, praying no one had heard that exchange. She also hoped it didn't cost her this job. Despite Erik, she enjoyed working here. She would even like Erik if he would quit asking her out and just be her boss.

"That was an interesting bit of interplay," Maddy said as she slipped into Jazmyn's office and closed the door. "I can't believe that man. He's never acted that way with anyone else."

"I don't know what it is." Jazmyn sank into her chair. "I don't know how to stop him, either. He's Kirsten's brother, so I don't want to complain to her."

"Maybe I can be discreet and say something."

Jazmyn gave her a pointed look.

"Okay, so maybe I'm not the most discreet person in the world. At least it's better than me practicing my martial arts on the guy." She posed in a mock karate stance.

Jazmyn couldn't help laughing. "Maddy, you don't know any martial arts."

"That's true." Maddy straightened her blouse. "But I learned from my mother how to swing a mean rolling pin. Maybe I'll bring one to work with me." She turned to the door and then grinned over her shoulder at Jazmyn. "If I use the rolling pin to knock him out, can I play the nurse and kiss him to make him feel better?"

"You're hopeless." Jazmyn waved her friend out the door. She glanced at the clock and saw it was time to meet Thor. Striding down the hall to the elevator, she tried to slow her pulse. Anticipation made her want to race down the stairs.

❧

Relaxing in the shade across from the T.L. Enterprises building, Thor wanted to shout up at Jazmyn to hurry. He wanted to see her. He wanted to know if her face would light up with a smile when she saw him. He wanted to know if she cared about him as much as he cared about her.

Last week at the party Kirsten and Erik hosted for the

employees, he'd watched Jazmyn from a place where no one could see him. She'd been stunning in a green dress that he knew almost matched the deep green of her eyes. How he'd longed to be close to her, to touch her, to kiss her again.

The door swung open. Jazmyn stepped out, and Thor crossed the street. She smiled when she saw him.

"Ready to go?" He almost couldn't think.

"Yep." She touched his arm. "First stop is the deli. I've ordered us a picnic lunch that we can take to the park."

A thrill shot through him. She wanted to be alone with him. She'd thought about what he would like and planned this just for him.

"Instead of the park, why don't we go to a pretty spot I know about." He glanced at his watch. "I know it's a little late, but we could be there in half an hour. Can you wait that long?"

"I'm fine." She gave him a mischievous smile. "I ordered some brownies. We could share one on the way to stave off hunger."

"That sounds like a plan to me." Thor had to fight the urge to pull her close and kiss her.

When they arrived at the little canyon, he couldn't help feeling pleased at Jazmyn's exclamations of delight. She was like a little child on an outing for the first time. He wanted to sit back and enjoy her excitement.

"Oh, a waterfall!" Jazmyn covered her mouth with her hands. Her eyes shone as she turned to Thor. "It's not as big as the one near your cabin, but it's beautiful. Can we eat over there on the rocks next to the water?"

"You read my mind, lady." Thor swung the basket from the truck and took Jazmyn's hand in his. "Be careful where you step."

They spread the lunch out on a boulder and sat on a flat rock across from it. Jazmyn had ordered sandwiches, potato salad, lemonade, and brownies. She'd even remembered what Thor ordered the last time so she could get what he wanted.

Thor's stomach rumbled. "I guess that's my signal to start eating." He paused. "Do you want to pray first?"

Jazmyn seemed surprised but pleased. When they'd been camping, he hadn't thought about prayer. He hadn't prayed at mealtimes since his mother passed away. She'd been the one who insisted they all attend church and who read stories to them from the Bible.

The food disappeared fast. Thor was glad to see Jazmyn eating. Sometimes at camp he'd thought the squirrels and chipmunks ate more than she did.

"How's the job?" He tried to act casual.

"It's okay."

"Problems?"

She leaned back against the rock next to him, staring at the waterfall. "There's this guy at work."

"Is he bothering you, or do you want to tell me to get lost because of him?" Thor was almost afraid to hear the answer. She hadn't encouraged Erik, but that could be because she wanted to say good-bye to Thor first.

"No. I mean, I don't want him to bother me. That's the trouble. He keeps asking me out."

"Can't you tell him you're not interested?"

"Believe me, I've tried." She sighed and plucked a blade of grass. "He doesn't seem to take the hint, and I've been pretty up-front about it."

"Why don't you talk to your boss about him?"

"That's part of the problem." Jazmyn frowned. "This guy is the boss. He's been out of the country for a while. Maybe he'll leave again soon."

She jerked the blade of grass in half. "He even had the nerve to suggest I might want to go out with him because of his money. A couple of times he's tried to give me little gifts, but I wouldn't take them."

Thor wanted to duck away in shame. Hearing Jazmyn, he wondered how he could have doubted her. She had a whole different set of values from the women he'd been involved with before. He had to stop this charade soon. The problem was, if he told her now, what would she do?

"You know, I even liked this guy the first time I met him. He seemed so nice. I guess you don't see a person's true colors right away." She looked up at him and smiled. "Look at you. I thought you were a murderer the first time I saw you. I wouldn't have guessed what a decent person you are."

Thor cleared his throat. "You never know why a person does things sometimes. Give this guy another chance. Maybe he'll turn out to be decent after all."

Jazmyn looked so dejected he couldn't resist putting his arm around her. She leaned her head against his shoulder. Contentment flowed over him. He stayed quiet, thinking he could sit like this with her forever.

This morning he'd called Jason and set up an appointment to see him tonight. He had to find out more about these beliefs Jason and Jazmyn shared with his mother. Then he could talk to Jason about the dilemma he'd gotten himself into. He'd deceived Jazmyn for so long he wasn't sure she would understand when he told her the truth about everything.

They sat so still that a few blue jays flew down to peck at the leftover crumbs from their lunch. The birds fought and chased one another until he and Jazmyn laughed aloud, scaring them away.

"I'd better get back to town." Thor stood up and helped Jazmyn to her feet. "I have an appointment tonight." With his arms still around her he couldn't resist one sweet kiss that left him longing for more.

seventeen

Standing outside the small house, Thor rubbed his palms on his pant legs. When he'd arranged this meeting with Jason, he'd been so sure he wanted to talk about this. Now he wanted to be anywhere but here. Some force urged him to run far and fast.

He clenched his jaw and rang the bell. The sound echoed in the house. He heard footsteps approaching. Too late. The door swung open.

"Thor, glad to see you." Jason held open the door, gesturing for him to come inside. "Please excuse the mess. I only got back two days ago, and I haven't finished unpacking." He led the way through a maze of gear and photography equipment to a small kitchen.

"Coffee?" Thor nodded, and Jason grabbed two mugs from a cabinet. He filled them and carried them to the table. "I can't believe how time gets mixed up when you travel around like this."

For the first time, Thor noticed Jason's rumpled appearance. His hair had grown out quite a bit in the last few weeks.

"I've heard of teens paying good money for a hairdo like that." Thor couldn't help grinning.

Jason ran a hand over his mop. "Yeah, I guess you're right. Where I was they didn't have any barbershops. I didn't trust the men wielding knives that close to my throat." He grimaced. "I'll have to get it cut tomorrow before Jazmyn sees me. She'll think I'm turning into a sixties hippie or something."

"So where did you go for this photo shoot?" Thor knew he

was grasping at anything to postpone the conversation he'd come here for.

"All over. I've been to so many places in the last month, I wasn't sure I'd know home when I got here." He took a swig from his mug and sighed. "We were mostly in Africa. There are more countries there than I can name. Did you know that?"

Thor chuckled. "I looked at a map once."

"Well, I am glad to be home. I think I could sleep for a week, though."

"I've heard jet lag is pretty tiring." Thor took a sip of coffee and tried not to grimace.

"Sorry about the brew." Jason lifted his mug. "I got home and didn't have any of the good stuff, so I'm using some Jazmyn left here. I've been too tired and too busy to get out to the store. Did you know Jazmyn got a job at the place you recommended? She loves it."

"I've been in town a couple of times since you left. I ran into Jazmyn, and we had lunch together. She did seem happy."

"I doubt you just stopped by to chat, Thor. What's up?" Jason's intense stare made Thor uncomfortable. He didn't know how to bring up the subject of religion now that he was here. All those burning questions had flown out of his head.

Shoving his chair back from the table, he crossed to the back door and stared out at the small yard. The grass was long and full of weeds. Everything had a look of neglect, which reflected Jason's having been gone for so long.

"I'm having trouble sleeping, living." He rubbed the back of his neck. "I don't know how to say why I came here. I needed to talk about something, but now I can't seem to remember why."

"This wouldn't have to do with some of the talks we had in the mountains, would it?" Jason asked.

"Yeah, I guess it does." Thor leaned against the door facing

Jason. "My mother believed like you do. She prayed all the time, took us to church. Her last words to me were that she had prayed for years that I would give my life to Jesus. She was dying with the hope that someday I would do what I needed to do."

Jason stayed quiet.

"All those times you talked, I tried to ignore you. I kept hearing my mother's voice echoing what you said. It won't let me go. I don't know what to do. I feel like someone's following me around whispering things in my ear that I can't quite make out. I think I'm going crazy. I've been living a lie. I can't do it anymore."

Jason shook his head. "You do have Someone whispering in your ear, you know. You're not crazy." Thor stared at him. Jason grinned. "The Spirit of God convicts us of our need for Jesus. You have a lot of people praying for you."

"So what am I supposed to do?" Thor crossed back to the chair, sank down, and rested his head on his hands.

"Have you considered giving your life to Jesus, Thor?"

"Yes. I keep hearing my mother's words, but I don't know how to do this. I'm sure she told me, but it's been so long." He swallowed hard against the lump clogging his throat.

Thor listened as Jason began to talk about sin and Jesus paying a debt on the cross. As Jason talked Thor could recall his mother saying some of these same things to him long ago, but he hadn't been ready to listen then. Now he wanted to take the next step beyond listening. He had a weight inside that wouldn't be relieved any other way. He didn't know how he knew this, but it was true.

As they prayed together tears streamed down Thor's cheeks. He couldn't remember the last time he'd cried, but he wasn't embarrassed. The weight lifted. Something indescribable washed over him.

Jason's eyes glistened when Thor looked up after the prayer. They both smiled, but Thor couldn't think of anything to say for a moment. His heart was too full. Jason seemed to understand. He refilled their cups and they drank in silence.

"Before I go I need to ask your advice." Thor shifted, uncomfortable again. "I've been sort of lying to you and Jazmyn."

"Lying how?"

Thor told him all of it. That he owned T.L. Enterprises. That he only worked as a hunting guide to stay away from the city. That he'd been duped by three women after his money and power. That he'd fallen in love with Jazmyn but didn't know how to tell her who he really was.

"Sounds to me like you've been running away for a long time." Jason traced a pattern in some coffee drips on the table. "You need to make things right. Talk to Jazmyn. Tell her who you are and why you deceived her."

"What if she hates me?" Thor wanted to take back the childish-sounding words.

"She may be hurt, but give her some time. Part of the reason you did this was because you didn't trust Jazmyn. That will hurt her. She'll need time. Be ready to give it to her."

Jason followed Thor to the door, slapping him on the back. "You're my brother in Christ. I'll stick up for you and put in a good word."

❧

"Hey, girlfriend." Maddy waved at Jazmyn as she crossed the garage to the elevator. The door whooshed open and Maddy held it, waiting for Jazmyn to catch up.

"Thanks, Maddy."

"You're running late this morning."

"I went to the gym early and lost track of time." Jazmyn was still trying to catch her breath.

"Why would you want to go before work?"

"There's been someone coming in the afternoons." Jazmyn wished the elevator would move faster. "I wanted to avoid them."

"Them, or him?" Maddy smirked. "I think I smell a good story here."

"What. Are you getting a job as a reporter?" Jazmyn put one hand on her hip and tried to imitate Maddy. They both laughed as the elevator doors slid open.

"If this is as juicy as I suspect, I may start an in-house newspaper," Maddy said, grinning. "Come on, let's continue this in your office. I don't want anyone else to scoop me."

"I won't say a word until I have some coffee. I didn't have time to stop anywhere on the way from the gym."

"You drive a hard bargain." Maddy shook her head. "Get prepared to talk. I'll stow my purse, get the coffee going, and be right back. I'll even see if I can scrape up something to eat since you probably didn't stop for any of that, either."

Jazmyn couldn't help smiling. "Maddy, you're a gem."

Flicking on her computer, Jazmyn ran through the messages on her desk, putting them in order of importance. This would be a busy day, but she liked it that way. Working hard would keep her mind off her troubles.

"Here we go." Maddy came in carrying a tray with two coffees and a couple of muffins. "I swiped these muffins from Kirsten's box. You'd better enjoy them. She isn't in yet, so I've got a few minutes."

Taking a sip of hot coffee, Jazmyn closed her eyes and leaned back in the chair. "I don't know how you do it, Maddy. You seem to know what I want before I do."

"I'm into bribes, girl." She plopped down across from Jazmyn. "So give."

"I don't know." Jazmyn hesitated, uncomfortable.

"Does this have anything to do with Kirsten's hunky

brother who's been following you around like an infatuated puppy dog?"

"Has he been that obvious?"

"Girlfriend, the whole office is buzzing about it. Makes all us single girls want to try on your shoes for a while."

"I would gladly give you my shoes. I'm not interested, but he doesn't seem to get the picture."

Maddy tilted her head. "I think I hear the boss. I'd better go. We'll talk about this later."

The morning passed quickly. Jazmyn had given up on getting any lunch when Maddy poked her head in the door. "Kirsten says we're ordering from the deli and having it delivered. Do you want your usual?"

"Sounds good. Make mine with a layer of caffeine or something that will give me an energy boost. Otherwise I may not make it through the afternoon."

"That'll teach you to work out early." Maddy clicked her tongue as she shut the door.

ஐ

Lunch hadn't had time to settle when Maddy swung into the office, slammed the door, and placed her hand over her heart.

"Maddy, what's wrong?" Jazmyn stared at the drama unfolding in front of her.

"I'm dying. You won't believe what just happened."

"I think you'd better sit down before you faint." Jazmyn pointed her pencil at the chair. "Take note that I'm way too busy to call the paramedics for you."

"He's here." Maddy gasped. She slid into a chair, her eyes wide.

"Who?"

"The missing owner I told you about. You won't believe this one. He's beyond hunk status."

"So who is he? Why's he finally here?" Jazmyn shuffled

through her papers trying to find a certain drawing. She'd stopped paying much attention to Maddy's theatrics. She had work to finish up.

"I thought Erik was cute, but I found out this is another brother of Kirsten's. He's even bigger than Erik and looks like some Norse god or something. Jazmyn, you have to see him. You won't believe it. I think I'm in love."

"Maddy, you're in love with someone new every two days." Jazmyn couldn't help smiling. "I keep telling you that love isn't based on looks."

"Well, if it was, this is the one I'd want to look at for the rest of my life." Maddy eased the door open and peeked out. "Quick." She motioned with her hand, her voice an exaggerated whisper. "Girlfriend, you have to see this."

Jazmyn sighed. There was no heading her off. The only thing that would satisfy Maddy would be for her to come and look at the latest hunk. At this point she was even willing to drool a little just so Maddy would leave her alone. She stepped to the door and started to pull it open.

"No," Maddy hissed, pulling Jazmyn to the other side. "Don't let him see you. I've heard he's as spooky as a wild animal."

A rumble of voices could be heard in the hall. One in particular struck a chord in Jazmyn. She knew that voice. She leaned her head next to Maddy's and peered out, feeling like a teenage girl spying on boys.

Kirsten and Erik stood in the hallway talking to another man whose back was to Jazmyn's office. He reminded her of someone she knew.

"Just wait until he turns around," Maddy whispered in her ear.

As if he'd heard, the man turned to glance at her office. Maddy eased the door closed, but not before Jazmyn got a good look at his face. The man talking to Kirsten and Erik was Thor. Her Thor.

"Maddy, that's not the owner of this company. He's the friend of my brother's that I had lunch with."

Maddy's eyes widened. "I'm telling you he is the head of this place. Kirsten introduced me to him just before I came in here."

The air in the room congealed around Jazmyn. She had trouble breathing. Thor was not the owner. He was a simple hunting guide. He wouldn't have lied to her.

The door to her office swung open. Thor faced her with Kirsten and Erik at his back.

eighteen

"Jazmyn, I need to talk to you." Thor stood in the door to her office, flanked by his brother and sister. Kirsten's assistant, as she'd been introduced, stood near Jazmyn, her eyes wide as saucers. Thor ignored her. His whole attention trained on Jazmyn, whose white face and glittering eyes made him wonder if she were about to faint.

"You lied to me. You're a fraud." It wasn't Jazmyn's words but the tone of despair that cut Thor.

"You really do know him?" Maddy was staring at Jazmyn now. "I thought you were joking."

"I thought I knew him." Jazmyn took a step back. "But I guess I was wrong." She lifted her chin, her green eyes darkened and cloudy like a storm-tossed sea. "Would you please leave my office? I have work to do."

"Not until we talk," Thor growled as he took a step toward her.

"No." She held up one hand. He stopped. "I don't want to talk to you."

"Jazmyn, I talked to Jason. He understands."

"I sincerely doubt that. Jason hates lying as much as I do." She rounded the desk, opened a drawer, and grabbed her purse. "If you won't leave, I will."

She edged around the other side of Maddy as if she were afraid Thor would leap forward and attack her.

"Jazmyn." Kirsten blocked the door.

"I'm sorry, Kirsten. I know we have a lot to do today. I promise I'll come in early and make it up to you." A tear escaped. Jazmyn swiped at her cheek. "Excuse me. I need to leave."

She tried to dart out the door, but Erik caught her and pulled her to him. "Jazmyn, please, give him a chance."

"Let me go, Erik." A small sob racked her. "I can see you were part of this deception, too. You must have had a great time laughing at me. All of you." She shot Kirsten an accusing look over her shoulder.

Kirsten raised her hand, opening her mouth to protest, but Jazmyn was gone. Thor listened in stunned silence as the elevator door dinged. This hadn't gone at all as he'd planned. If Kirsten and Erik hadn't waylaid him and introduced him around, he would have been in Jazmyn's office before anyone could alert her that he was here.

"I'm sorry, Thor." Kirsten placed her hand on his arm. "Give her some time. She's just hurt right now."

Heaviness filled Thor. He wasn't angry; he was afraid. For the first time he'd found a woman he could trust, and he'd betrayed that trust. How could this ever be resolved? How could he make Jazmyn understand why he'd done what he had done?

"I need to go. I'll try to find her." Thor hadn't the vaguest idea where to look for Jazmyn. He had the feeling she wouldn't go home, but where would she go?

As if she could read his mind, Kirsten whirled to face her secretary. "Maddy, do you know where Jazmyn would go?"

"I'm not sure. You could check the gym, but she already went there once today." She shrugged. "She likes coffee. Maybe she went somewhere close by to grab a cup."

"Thanks." Thor squeezed Kirsten's shoulders and headed for the door.

"Thor." He turned back to see what Kirsten wanted. "If I see her, I'll try to talk to her. Do I have your permission to say anything about why you did this?"

He hesitated. In order for her to understand, Jazmyn would have to be told, but he hated that thought. He gave a short nod. "Tell her."

"Do you want me to go with you?" Erik took a step as if to follow him. "I know she doesn't think highly of me right now, but I could at least help look."

"No. Thanks." Thor strode down the hall to the elevator, wondering what he should do now. This afternoon certainly hadn't gone as he'd planned.

Outside the sky had clouded over, matching his mood. He wanted to go off into the woods and walk for hours. If he had Loki or Odin here with him, maybe they could track Jazmyn down. He'd left them at the house and didn't want to take the time to get them. Where would she go?

The gym wasn't far. He decided to walk, stopping by the coffee shops on the way to see if she might be in one of them. She wasn't in any of those places, and she wasn't at the gym. On the way back to the T.L. building, he thought of checking the garage. Quickening the pace, he hurried past the rows of cars until he reached the space designated for Jazmyn. Her car was gone. He felt like kicking something. Hard. Why hadn't he thought to check here before going off on a wild goose chase down the street?

Hurrying to his truck, Thor revved the engine and sped from the garage, ignoring the glare from the guard. Where would she go? Home? To the mall? He didn't think Jazmyn was the type of woman to drown her sorrows in a shopping spree. He turned away from the mall toward her apartment building.

Thor pounded so hard on Jazmyn's door that he was surprised it didn't crash open. He hadn't seen her car in the parking lot, but he hoped she might have parked elsewhere to fool him. She wasn't home. He slumped against the wall beside her door. He was running out of places to look.

Jason. Once again Thor wanted to kick himself. Of course, she would go to her brother when she'd been hurt like this. They were so close. Jason would be able to pray with her.

Prayer. Why hadn't he thought to pray? Wasn't that what Christians were supposed to do? Pray about everything? Thor shook his head. Maybe he wasn't a real Christian after all. He sure hadn't thought about talking to God over this situation. He hadn't even prayed this afternoon before he went to see Jazmyn. What kind of Christian would make a mistake like that?

Relief flooded him when he saw Jazmyn's car parked in Jason's driveway. She was here. He'd found her. He realized a small part of him had been concerned that she'd done something reckless. Knowing she was safe brought great peace of mind.

The frown on Jason's face as he opened the door told Thor he might not be welcome right now. He opened his mouth to speak, but Jason held up his hand to stop him.

"Yes, she's here, Thor. No, you can't see her."

"I have to talk to her, Jason. She's got to understand."

"She won't understand a thing right now. She's been hurt too bad." Jason's look and his tone softened. "Thor, you lied to her. All her life, our mother told her all men lie. She'd started to believe Mom was wrong before you did this. Go back home, Thor. Give her some time."

Thor stared at the door as Jason closed it. He wanted to force it open. He had to see Jazmyn. Instead, he turned and trudged down the walkway to his truck.

❧

Stepping off the elevator, Jazmyn felt her heart pounding. She half expected Thor to be waiting to pounce on her. She hadn't been to work in two days. She wanted to quit, but

Jason convinced her not to. When Kirsten called and begged her to come back, Jazmyn relented. Kirsten promised Thor wouldn't bother her at work, but Jazmyn hadn't been sure that would stand. After all, he was the owner.

"Hey, girlfriend. Good to see you." Maddy came flying out of her office and enveloped Jazmyn in a hug.

Maddy stepped back, her hands still holding Jazmyn's shoulders, her gaze penetrating. "You okay? I'd say you haven't been sleeping. Those circles under your eyes get any darker, people will mistake you for a raccoon."

"I'm fine." Jazmyn almost choked on the words.

"Come on. I'll get some coffee and go over the pile on your desk with you. Kirsten's gone for the day, but she's given you enough work to keep you busy for forty-eight hours straight. She must be from the school of thought that hard work is good for the lovesick."

"I'm not lovesick." Jazmyn couldn't help feeling a little better around Maddy. The woman could talk a person to death, but she was a sweetheart. Jazmyn hadn't realized how much she missed her.

The day sped by. Jazmyn had expected to have trouble at work, but she was so busy she didn't have time to consider her woes. Although she hadn't realized it before, work was exactly what she needed to take her mind off Thor.

A week passed before the workload slowed down. Thor called her twice, but she was out of the office both times. He said he'd gone back to his cabin in the mountains so she could have some time. He didn't want to push. He wanted her to know how sorry he was for what he'd done.

Jazmyn refused to talk to anyone about what had happened. She didn't try to contact Thor. When Jason said he had something important to tell her concerning Thor, she brushed him off, refusing to listen.

Sleep eluded her. She lost weight. Every time she looked at food she recalled the lunches she'd shared with Thor and the way love had slipped into their relationship. At least on her part. Maybe what happened was God's way of separating them since Thor wasn't a believer. She told herself that often, hoping to be convinced it was the truth.

"Jazmyn, it's lunchtime." Kirsten smiled from the doorway. "Would you go with me? I have something I need to discuss with you, and my afternoon schedule is filled."

"Sure. Let me get my purse and my notebook." Jazmyn pushed back from her desk and stood, stretching the kinks out before she grabbed her things.

"I have no idea how we managed before you came to work here." Kirsten led the way to the elevator. "You've taken such a load off of me."

Kirsten had reservations at a little bistro where the hostess led them to a private table. Jazmyn slipped into her chair and tried not to stare around her. She'd never been in such a fancy restaurant.

Kirsten kept the conversation light as they nibbled at bread and ate their salads. When Jazmyn couldn't eat another bite, she pulled out her notebook.

"You won't need that." Kirsten pushed her plate away. "I wanted to talk to you about my brother."

Dread sent a chill through Jazmyn. "I'd rather not." She could feel the lump growing in her throat. "I enjoyed the lunch, but we'd better get back." She started to get up.

"Sit down, Jazmyn." Kirsten gave her a sad smile. "I don't usually assert my authority as boss, but this time I must. I've watched you this last week. You've worked like a maniac, and you look terrible. This can't go on."

Jazmyn blinked and stared down at her plate. Part of her wanted to storm out of the restaurant. The other part wanted to stay, to hear what Kirsten had to say.

"Will you listen? Please?" Kirsten's fingers closed over Jazmyn's and she gave a light squeeze. Jazmyn nodded, not trusting her voice to work.

Kirsten sighed. "I've thought about this. I wasn't even sure where to begin. Thor was such a bright child. He succeeded in school and in every business venture he tried from the time he was six and had a lemonade stand. He had every parent on our street stopping to get a drink. In college he could do no wrong. That was where he got the idea for T.L." She gave Jazmyn a sad smile. "By the way, that stands for Thor Larson."

Jazmyn's eyes widened. It had been there all the time if she'd only put it together. After all, Thor was the one who recommended she try for a job there.

"Thor's business succeeded beyond his wildest expectations. He suddenly had more money and power than any young man his age should have. I'm afraid it went to his head, although he, of course, didn't realize it.

"He began to date a young woman who fawned over him. Erik and I could see that she was a gold digger, but Thor was blinded. To make a long story short, she almost had him at the altar before he discovered her true colors."

Jazmyn blinked back tears again, this time for what had happened to Thor. She started to speak, but Kirsten held up her hand.

"He didn't learn easily. The same thing happened to him twice more before he gave up on being in control. He turned the outward running of the company over to Erik and me. He went off to the mountains and became a hermit. He swore he would have nothing to do with another woman." She blew out a breath as she watched Jazmyn. "He kept that vow until he met you. He didn't tell you who he was because he was afraid."

Jazmyn wanted to say something, but the words wouldn't

come. All this time she'd thought he was playing her for the fool, but he was afraid of what she'd do to him.

"Give yourself some time to heal, Jazmyn. I'm sure you need that." Kirsten gathered her things and stood. "I don't like to interfere, but I hate seeing you and my brother hurting like this when I care about both of you so much."

nineteen

Insistent banging. Jazmyn cracked one eye open. Seven in the morning. Saturday morning. Her day to sleep in.

"This better be good." She searched near the bed for her slippers as she pulled on her robe. "This better be a matter of grave importance." She glanced in the hallway mirror and groaned.

Jason waited outside her door, bouncing with impatience. As she opened the door, she gave him a scathing look, designed to intimidate an army general. Jason grinned.

"Whoa. Where's my camera when I need it?" He snorted a laugh. "Of course, right now you'd probably break the lens."

"Nice to see you. Come back later." Jazmyn started to close the door, but she wasn't quick enough.

"Wait a minute, Sis." He stuck his briefcase in the door, then pushed his way into her apartment. "You're going to be glad I came over here."

"I can't imagine that happening this early." Jazmyn yawned.

"Tell you what." Jason turned her in the direction of her bedroom. "Why don't you go wake up and get dressed. I'll fix coffee and see what I can drum up for breakfast."

She trudged back down the hall feeling a little better. At least if someone had to wake her up, it was nice to have him fix breakfast.

Her hair still damp from the shower, Jazmyn wandered to the kitchen, following the delicious smells. Jason must have heard her coming, because he had a cup of coffee waiting for her on the table. Two places were set, and a plate of toast stood between them. She leaned over, breathing in the fragrant aroma of cinnamon hazelnut.

"Well, you do clean up nice." Jason carried plates with omelets to the table. "There for a minute I thought you were on your deathbed. I almost dialed 911."

"You know better than to come over here this early on a Saturday." Jazmyn snagged a piece of toast for her plate, then took her first bite of omelet. "I didn't even know I had these ingredients in the refrigerator. How did you do it?"

"That would be my secret." Jason winked. "A guy can't give up all his secrets, you know."

Jason inhaled his breakfast. While she chewed and savored, he cleared his place and retrieved his briefcase. When he opened it on the table, a receipt fluttered out, coming to rest beside Jazmyn's plate.

"Secret, huh?" She gave him a disgusted look as she read the omelet ingredients on the grocery receipt dated this morning.

He looked sheepish. "Well, I wasn't sure what you'd have available. You don't cook much. I figured you'd at least have eggs, so the rest was easy."

"You must be sweetening me up for something. What is it?"

He laughed. "Actually, I have some rather good news, and I wanted to make sure you were awake and ready before I sprang it on you."

"Good news?"

Like a little boy eager to bring out his best show-and-tell, Jason reached into the briefcase and drew out some papers. "Look at this." He handed them to her.

Jazmyn's brow furrowed as she studied the form he'd given her. "What is this?"

"It's a contract." If he smiled any wider, his face would split. "I sent a few of the drawings you made at camp to my editor.

He wants to include them in my book. You'll get some advance and a small percentage of the royalties. It isn't much, but I thought you'd like it."

She stared at the contract. Her drawings? In a book? "How did you? They really liked them?" She couldn't seem to make a coherent thought. Thor had suggested this, but she hadn't taken him seriously. She hadn't thought Jason would, either.

"I took a few from the drawing book. I didn't think you'd miss them." Jason looked anxious. "He wants to see more of the sketches. If you want, that is."

Grabbing the papers away from her, Jason thumbed through them until he came to a page of photographs and sketches. "See, this is what they plan to do. Your drawings will be sort of whimsical additions to my photographs." He was right. This picture of an elk racing across a field also had a sketch of Xena on a pine branch, scolding whoever had offended her.

Tears sprang to her eyes. "This is wonderful, Jason. Thank you." She jumped up from her chair and gave him a bear hug.

"Now that I've gotten you all softened up, are you ready for what else I have to tell you?"

She stepped back, suspicious. "Out with it."

"I have to go back for a few more photos. You need to come and do some more sketches, too. My editor would like some of your work on almost every page." He fiddled with the papers still in his briefcase. "I'll call Thor and arrange for another week. Can you get off work?"

"No." She backed away until she came up against the counter. "I don't want to go up there again."

"Is it because of Thor, or because you don't want to camp?"

"I. . .I loved the camping. I just can't be around him, Jason. You don't understand." She crossed her arms over her stomach, digging her fingers into her sides. "I can't be around him."

"Jaz, why?" Jason crossed to stand near her. "Do you dislike him so much? Are you still mad?"

"No." Her brain fumbled for a way to explain without saying too much. "I talked to Kirsten, his sister. Or rather she talked to me. Thor has a reason from his past that made him do what he did. I can understand, and I forgave him."

"Then what is it? I thought you liked him."

"I. . .I can't be around him." She couldn't think of anything more to say.

Jason chuckled. "I get it. You like him. In fact, I would guess you think you like him too much. Is that right?"

Her face warmed. "He's not a Christian, Jason. I have to stay away from him."

"Ahhh." Jason's eyes twinkled. "I guess he didn't get the chance to tell you about his visit with me. That's why he came to see you at the office that day, to tell you who he really is."

"What visit? What are you talking about?"

"The night before you saw Thor at T.L. Enterprises, he came to my house and asked me how to become a Christian. We talked, and he prayed to receive Christ. He's a Christian now, Jazmyn. Does that make a difference?"

"A Christian?" She couldn't breathe. Thor was a Christian. She could tell him she forgave him. There would be no barriers between them. Tears of joy moistened her eyes.

"So will you go with me again?" Jason asked.

Jazmyn thought of the smell of the pines, the ripple of the river, Xena the squirrel, and Thor. They seemed to fit together in the outdoors, and she realized she loved them all. "I'll ask Kirsten if I can get the week off. I don't know if she'll let me since I haven't worked there that long."

"My guess is that if she knows you're going to mend bridges with her brother, she'll let you go." Jason gave her a quick hug. "This time, be sure to pack heavy clothes. The weather will be even cooler in the mountains now."

Jazmyn smiled as she thought of snuggling up to Thor and letting him help her stay warm. She couldn't wait.

ða

"For the life of me I don't understand why you're back in town, Thor." Kirsten sounded exasperated as she leaned against her husband, Wes, on the couch. They were trying to watch a movie, but Thor knew he was distracting them. His constant pacing and prowling around the room had to be annoying.

"She's right. You're acting like a tiger in a cage." Erik tossed a piece of popcorn into his mouth. "What brought you back to town, anyway?"

"Nothing." Thor stalked to the back door and stared out at the dark yard. How could he explain that he hoped to see Jazmyn and talk to her again? He wanted to tell her he was sorry. Maybe he'd dreamed of her forgiving him and falling into his arms.

He turned back into the room and flopped down in an overstuffed chair. How many times had he been up and down this evening? He was acting like a lovesick animal.

He paused in his thoughts. That was the problem, wasn't it? He loved Jazmyn, but she hated him for what he'd done to her. Her mother had told her all men were worthless liars. Is that what she thought of him?

Thor wanted to pace the floor again. He started to get up, but one dagger glare from Kirsten froze him in place. What could he do? Jazmyn didn't want to see him. Kirsten advised him to give her more time before he approached her. How long did a man have to wait?

"I'm going out." He ignored his jacket on the way to the door. Up in the mountains he needed a coat by nightfall. Here in the valley the temperature was still mild.

He wound through side streets, taking his time to think, to plan what he would say. He recognized his need for someone to help him, but asking would be hard. By the time he pulled up in front of the small house and cut the engine, he thought he knew exactly how he would approach this.

When Jason opened the door every argument Thor had planned flew out of his head. This was Jazmyn's brother. He was probably angry with him, too.

Instead of slamming the door in Thor's face, Jason swung it wide, a welcoming smile on his face. "Thor. I tried to call that number you gave me, but your phone was off. I was going to drive up to see you tomorrow."

"Me?" Thor stepped inside, dread making him want to run. Had Jason wanted to chew him out?

"Yeah, it's about my book." Jason led the way to the kitchen. "Coffee? Soda?"

Thor couldn't imagine Jason offering him something to drink if he planned to yell at him. He began to relax. "A cola would be nice."

Jason filled a glass with ice, popped the tab on a cola can, and set them in front of Thor.

"I need to go back to the mountains for some more pictures to round out my book. The editor gave me some specifics. He wants me to have them ready within three weeks. I wondered if you would be able to guide for me again."

"You shouldn't go up there right now." Thor stared at Jason. Didn't he realize what time of year this was?

"Why not?"

"This is hunting season. Do you know how many irresponsible hunters there are in the mountains where we were?"

Jason looked perplexed. "But you guide them. You should be familiar enough with the favorite areas to keep us safe."

"I don't like it." Thor frowned. "You have to stay still for too long. Besides, the animals are much harder to find. They're spooked right now. It doesn't take long after the season opens to have them running at the sound of a pin dropping."

"Then we'll have to be quiet. My editor gave me this deadline. I'll go do the photos with or without you. With you would be much easier."

"It's just too dangerous. I can't take you." Thor knew he was being unreasonable, but he couldn't seem to help himself.

Jason tilted his head as he studied Thor. "You're not making any sense. What's the real reason you don't want to take me?"

Thor began to pace. He could see the light from the street lamps illuminating part of the yard while the rest was swathed in shadow. "I don't know. I feel like my life is a mess. I don't know what to do."

"Come sit down." Jason's tone softened. Thor could hear the caring. He crossed back to the kitchen chair and sank down.

"You know, quite often when a person first becomes a Christian, they face trials right away. That might be why you're so confused. Let's pray first, then we'll talk."

When Jason finished praying he squeezed Thor's arm. "Now tell me why you feel like your life is falling apart."

"Because I was living a lie. Now I have to pay the consequences. I thought I'd lost your friendship. I know I lost what I had with your sister."

"That's the real problem, isn't it?" Jason asked.

"Yeah. I'm crazy about her, Jason. I love her, but now she won't see me or even talk to me. Kirsten said to give her time, but that doesn't seem to be working, either." Thor hated the desperation in his voice, but he couldn't seem to stop. He felt as if a dam had broken inside.

"How much time have you given her, Thor? Some hurts go very deep." He sat back, running his hand through his hair. "I told you before that our mother soured Jazmyn on men for years. She did tell her that all men lied. She also told Jaz that all men leave eventually. When her fiancé, Adam, died, that's what Jazmyn thought—that he'd left her. A lot of people get angry at those who die for that very reason." He paused. "Anyway, when you lied to her it was like proving that the two main things Mom taught her were true. That will take time to get over."

He squeezed Thor's arm again. "I'm not saying she'll ever be more than friends with you, but you can pray about it. God can mend hurts and heal hearts."

twenty

Thor arrived at the camp early. Loki and Odin exploded from the truck when he opened the door. He drew in a deep breath, savoring the clean pine scent. He loved this place.

Last week he let Jason convince him to be the guide for this second photo shoot. There shouldn't be too much danger. They both knew enough to wear bright clothing. This spot was so isolated that few hunters came here. Being around Jason might bring Jazmyn to mind more often, but he thought about her all the time, anyway.

Pushing those thoughts aside, he began to unload and set up camp. By the middle of the afternoon he had the camp looking pretty good. He and the dogs had just returned from cutting wood when he heard a vehicle approaching. He tossed a log from the truck bed and hopped down to wait. This would be Jason coming.

He waved as Jason drove his SUV into the river crossing. Loki and Odin bounded forward, eager to greet the new-comer. Jason ground to a stop on the far side of camp. The dogs fell all over each other trying to get there first.

Thor strode across the camp to greet his friend and help him unpack. For the first time he noticed that a second per-son rode in the SUV. It was Jazmyn. Tousled and beautiful, she caught Thor's gaze. She stared at him. He could see something in her eyes. Was it hatred? Disgust? Jason hadn't said he would be bringing his sister this time, too.

Thor shook hands with Jason. He nodded at Jazmyn. "Need some help unloading and setting up?"

"I think we can manage if you have other stuff you're doing." Jason shrugged into a warm coat. "Brrr. I haven't been up here this time of year in a long time. I'd forgotten how chilly the air can be."

Thor grinned. "Not chilly, invigorating. Look at the dogs. They act like young pups when I bring them up this time of year."

Jason laughed. Bending over, he gave both dogs a good ear rubbing. "Any place in particular you want me to set up the tents?"

"Anywhere's fine. I'm going to finish with the wood so we can have a fire. That will be important tonight."

He stalked back to his truck, wondering how he would be able to manage a whole week around Jazmyn. After he and Jason had talked, Thor believed Jazmyn would never be able to love him as he loved her. He'd accepted that, but he didn't know how he could manage to be in her presence without letting her know how much he still loved her. Would always love her.

He'd been doing a lot of Bible study and prayer this past week, hoping to heal his bruised heart. For the first time he'd found a woman with values he admired. Now that he wasn't consumed with himself, he understood how shallow he'd been in his former relationships. As long as he stayed away from her, he might be able to love Jazmyn from afar. Being close wasn't going to work.

He threw the rest of the wood off the truck, then stacked the smaller pieces. Grabbing up the axe, he split the bigger logs, reveling in the feel of the strenuous labor. As he concentrated on chopping wood he tried to ignore Jazmyn as she helped Jason set up their tents.

From time to time she cast strange looks at him. Thor thought she might be as uncomfortable around him as he was around her. The solution to this problem had to be keeping busy. He would take Jason out from dawn to dusk. He only hoped Jazmyn wouldn't want to tag along. Having her in the truck next to him would be unbearable.

"Let me help you get this stacked." Jason wandered over as Thor finished splitting the wood. "Jazmyn is arranging her tent. Are you upset that I brought her?"

"You can bring anyone you want."

"I didn't tell you that she's doing some drawings for my book. My editor really liked her work."

Thor couldn't suppress his surprise. "You mean the sketches she did when we were up here before?"

"Yeah. I sent some in without her knowing it." Jason shrugged. "I thought it was worth a try."

"I still have the one she gave me. The picture of the baby skunk trying to fish marshmallows from the fire." Thor didn't tell Jason the sketch was framed, hanging on his workroom wall. Every time he saw it, he thought of Jazmyn and their time in the mountains. "She's so good at capturing the action of the animals. I'm glad they're using them."

"She plans to stay in camp while we go out for the pictures. That will give her plenty of time to draw." Jason picked up an armload of logs. "I wasn't sure if she'd be able to get off work, but your sister let her go. That was nice of her."

"Where do you want to start shooting?" Thor wanted to get off the subject of Jazmyn. "We could start over in the canyon we hiked and see if we can find the eagles. There might be some bear there this time of year."

"That sounds good." Jason paused as if thinking. Behind them, Thor heard the tent zipper. He braced himself. Jazmyn must be finished setting up her things. Would she want to join them?

"Ahhh!" she cried out. Something clanked loudly.

Jason and Thor both whirled around. Jazmyn's arms wind-milled as she fell back against the tent. The poles collapsed. The canvas gave, then sank to the ground. Jazmyn's feet flew up in the air before hitting the ground with a loud thud.

"Jazmyn!" Jason started to run. Thor passed him. He hadn't heard a shot, but they'd been talking. What if some hunter had sent a wild bullet their way?

A fold of the tent covered Jazmyn's face. She was shaking like a leaf. It must be from pain. Thor dropped to the ground on one side as Jason knelt across from him. Jason lifted the tent flap covering her features.

Tears ran down her cheeks.

"Jaz, where are you hurt?" Jason leaned closer.

"I'm not." She gasped out the words, her body still shaking. Jason looked at Thor as if they'd both realized in the same instant that Jazmyn wasn't hurt. She was laughing, not crying. She'd been clumsy, managed to knock down the tent, and thought it was hilarious. Thor couldn't help smiling as he climbed to his feet, leaving Jason to help his sister up.

&

Xena scampered out on a branch not far over Jazmyn's head. She knew the squirrel was eyeing the chocolate bar she'd placed on the arm of her chair. She wanted to tempt the squirrel so she would come out and go through her antics.

"Come on, sweetie. I need you to pose." Jazmyn sat with pencil poised as Xena's tail jerked upward.

Chattering noisily, Xena leaped for the trunk of the tree. She hopped a few steps, paused, cocked her head, and looked at Jazmyn as if to say, "Get away from my chocolate."

The pencil flew as Jazmyn tried to capture the spirit of the defiant squirrel. Xena had such personality. Within moments she'd finished. On the paper a very perturbed Xena stared up at her. Jazmyn wondered if the people who bought this book would understand that Xena wanted chocolate. She was almost willing to fight for it.

"Tell me, girl." Jazmyn set the pad down and picked up the candy bar. "Have you ever had any guy troubles?"

Xena skittered a few steps up the trunk and paused to watch as Jazmyn peeled away the wrapper. Her beady black eyes followed every movement, her body tensed, ready to grab and run.

"I would give you some of this, Xena, but you wouldn't believe the problems that can come from eating chocolate. What if you ended up fat because you ate too many candy bars?" Jazmyn broke off a bite. "You might not be able to fit into that little hole where you sleep in the winter. That would be a shame."

She stuck the bite in her mouth, savoring the sweetness. Xena skittered back down a couple of steps as if wondering where hers was.

"Think of this as my doing you a favor." Jazmyn wrapped the bar back up and stuck it in her pocket. Xena did not seem to appreciate the favor. She raced up to the branch. Her chattering and scolding startled a couple of birds.

Jazmyn laughed. "I think I'd like to learn that phrase to repeat to a certain man I know. He did something really mean to me. I'd be willing to talk about it and, after making him sweat, even forgive him." She sighed as Xena scampered farther up the tree. "Okay, I won't make him sweat. I'll forgive him, but he has to be willing to talk. So far we've been here four days, and he hasn't said anything to me that wasn't necessary."

She slammed her sketchpad shut and stared up the tree. "I could be a faceless robot and he wouldn't care." She clamped her lips together. This had to be the worst she'd ever been. Here she was, talking to an animal.

"Lord, You know what I'm trying to say. I listened to what

Kirsten told me about Thor. I didn't want to forgive him, but then I understood he hadn't meant to hurt me. He was protecting himself."

She stood and stretched. "I'd like to talk to him about it, but maybe I read his interest wrong. He doesn't seem to want to have anything to do with me. Unless I'm way off, I think he is sorry I came up here with Jason."

Placing her drawing book in the SUV, Jazmyn wandered down to the river. The steady ripple of the water soothed her. She'd love to have a house right here where she could listen to this sound every night as she was falling asleep. It would be better than counting sheep.

"Lord, I know I hurt him by being unreasonable, by not listening. Help me make that up to him somehow. Show me how." Jazmyn thought about Queen Esther in the Old Testament. Esther had waited patiently until the time was just right to speak to the king. She hadn't rushed in and started throwing out wild accusations. She'd demonstrated great wisdom and trust in the Lord to the point of putting her own life in jeopardy.

"Keep me from rushing in, Lord. I want to grab him and shake him. I know that's not Your plan." She bent down to retrieve a handful of pebbles. "Lord, these represent the things I want. I'm giving them all to You, relying on You to provide for my needs and to help me forget my wants." One at a time Jazmyn threw the pebbles into the river. Each time she thought of a selfish want that she'd been holding on to. When she finished she felt better. She would wait and see how the Lord worked.

She almost had supper finished when the guys returned. Jason began to sort and store his film. He would take the next half-hour to get his cameras put to bed, as he put it.

Loki and Odin rose and stretched, their tails wagging as

they watched Thor striding toward them.

Shadows were growing long already as the sun fell behind the trees. The fire had almost died out. Jazmyn had tried to build a new fire on the old coals, but it was more smoke than flames.

"I hope you don't mind that I started supper. I remembered your recipe for sloppy joes. At least, I think I got it right." Jazmyn bit her lip to stop from chattering. Thor looked grim and tired. He wouldn't want to be bothered with what she had to say.

He nodded at her. "Smell's good. I'll work on the fire." As he moved away, Jazmyn couldn't keep from watching him. She loved the graceful way he walked, as if he were aware of everything around him and prepared for anything. She imagined the Apaches who used to live here moved the same way.

During supper Jason kept up a running commentary on everything they'd seen that day. He told Jazmyn about the wild turkeys. She couldn't help but laugh as he described the way their heads kept popping up out of the grass they were hiding in.

"You'll never guess what else we saw today." Jason looked like a little boy about to burst at the seams with his news.

"Um. A deer." Jazmyn laughed as Jason rolled his eyes.

"We saw the wolves." He leaned forward, excitement shining in his eyes. He'd already told her about the program to reintroduce wolves in this area. Only a few had survived, so the chances of finding one were slim.

"Jason, that's wonderful." Jazmyn jumped up to give him a hug. She knew what this would mean to his editor.

"Tomorrow we're going to look for elk, but the next day we want to try to find the wolves again," Jason said. "If you have all your sketches done, maybe you can go along with us."

Thor pushed up from his chair. "If you'll excuse me, I'm

going to bed. Dawn comes early." Was he angry that Jason asked her to go with them? Did he dislike her so much that he couldn't stand the thought of being in the same vehicle with her?

Jazmyn sank back down. She stared at the crackling flames. *God, help me to be like Esther.*

twenty-one

Jazmyn's breath puffed out in a white cloud as she stuck her head out of the sleeping bag. Jason scratched on the side of the tent. He called to her for the second time.

"I'm awake." She shivered, drawing the bag tight around her shoulders. "This isn't funny, Jason. Even Santa Claus and his elves don't like it this cold."

"Just be glad we don't have six feet of snow to go with it." Jason slapped the tent. "Up and at 'em. Time to get moving. Thor's got coffee on. He's fixing some breakfast."

She groaned. It must be three hundred degrees below zero. "I shouldn't have been working out so much. It would have been smarter to put on blubber like a whale."

"Are you talking to yourself in there, Sis?"

"I'd never do such a thing." Jazmyn gritted her teeth, reaching for her clothes. The jeans and sweatshirt were so cold she almost couldn't bear to touch them, let alone put them on. The other mornings hadn't been this cold.

"I hope you kept your clothes in the sleeping bag last night so they're warm this morning." She could hear Jason walking away.

"Fine time to tell me," Jazmyn muttered under her breath. She snuggled back into the sleeping bag, hoping the clothes would warm up fast. At least she had her socks on, but her shoes were probably like blocks of ice.

A few minutes later she unzipped the tent and made a beeline for the fire. She stood close, feeling like a chicken on a spit as she rotated to warm her whole body.

Jason came over carrying a plate of hash browns and eggs. The thought of warm food set her stomach growling.

"Here, have a seat." He snagged a chair and pulled it close to the fire. Jazmyn sank into it. She accepted the plate from him. "Thor and I will be right over with ours."

Jazmyn waited until the men joined her. From the corner of her eye she watched Thor. She couldn't help it. Being close to him this week, without the rapport they'd shared before, had been sheer torture.

She'd also spent the week watching Thor to see if he'd changed at all. Did he become a Christian in name only as so many people did? She didn't think so. He was a strong person, a decision-maker, but from what she'd learned he hadn't always thought about how his decisions affected others. Although he still had the assertive traits, they now appeared to be tempered by consideration for others.

She wondered if that was why he stayed away from her. Maybe he thought she didn't want anything to do with him, so he was intent on not pushing her. Today she had to find a way to change that. She'd come to the realization that she loved him and didn't want to live without him.

"About done, Jaz?" Jason tossed his paper plate into the fire. "Good breakfast, Thor. Hit the spot."

Jazmyn stared at the bit of egg and mound of potatoes still on her plate. She didn't want to be rude, but if they were going over some of the rough roads they usually traveled looking for wildlife, she didn't want to eat too much.

"Don't worry about finishing." She looked up to find Thor standing beside her. "Done?" At her nod, he reached for her plate. "I'll leave the potatoes for our little friends."

He strode away from camp. Jazmyn couldn't stop watching him. Every time he spoke to her, her pulse sped up. She hoped this time he would warm up to her.

"If you drizzle chocolate over the potatoes, Xena will be yours forever." She almost clapped her hand over her mouth. Had she said that? Jason was laughing behind her.

Thor flashed her a smile, the first all week. "That's just what I need. A neurotic, chocolate-addicted female."

Warmth flooded through Jazmyn. Maybe they could get past the hurts. Maybe today Thor would open up to her. She needed to be patient, though. With the pushy women he'd been involved with before, he didn't need her to be pushy, too.

"Where are we going first?" Jazmyn asked as she climbed into the truck.

"I thought we'd head up to Hannigan's meadow area. We might find some bighorn sheep there. Then we'll circle back to Kettleholes. That's where we saw the wolves yesterday. Jason wanted to try to get a few more shots of them." Thor moved the truck to the side of the road to let a vehicle piled with hunters go past.

Jazmyn tried not to lean against Thor at all. The moment they'd shared in camp hadn't lasted. When she climbed in the truck next to him, she sensed he didn't want her to be there. She tried to ignore the hurt, but she kept wondering what had happened. He hadn't even given her the chance to apologize for the way she'd behaved when she learned his true identity. Perhaps she should have forced the issue, should have faced him down.

As they topped out at Hannigan's meadow, Thor slowed to turn onto a side road that was little more than a track. Nothing moved in the wide grassy area.

Back in the trees he pulled the truck off to the side and parked. "Okay, we walk from here."

The hike in the thin mountain air wasn't easy, but Jazmyn could tell her workouts at the gym were helping. She didn't feel like she would pass out at any moment as she had the last time.

Thor hunkered down. He motioned Jazmyn and Jason to come closer. As if he weren't thinking, he reached back, grasped Jazmyn's hand, and tugged her down beside him. Over the top of the brush she could see the mountain sheep. Two mothers were grazing about thirty yards away. As she watched, three babies bounded into view. Her breath caught at the beauty and grace of the animals. The young ones were almost too cute.

Beside Jazmyn, Jason brought up his camera. From the corner of her eye she could see him studying the angles, looking for the best shots. He motioned to Thor that he was moving around to a better spot. Jazmyn held her breath, hoping the sheep wouldn't see them and flee before Jason got the pictures he needed.

The babies looked as if they were playing tag, bounding uphill and down chasing one another. Jazmyn was reminded of cartoons she'd watched as a child when the sheep would leap stiff-legged from one place to another. She wanted to laugh out loud but couldn't.

She glanced down to find her fingers still entwined with Thor's. Looking up, she saw him gazing at her. He turned away, his hand releasing hers, but not before she saw the longing in his eyes. He did still love her. She was sure of it. Now she had to wait for the right time to act.

❧

Kneeling down, studying the wolf tracks, Thor knew they weren't far away. He knew the den would be close. By this time of year they would be teaching the young to hunt in the pack, preparing them for life on their own.

"This way." He spoke low, not in a whisper, because that might carry too far. Jazmyn and Jason caught up to him. They needed to hurry. They'd taken too long with the sheep, and now dusk was too close. Besides, they'd heard a gunshot not too far off. Thor didn't trust any hunter's accuracy in this light.

He tried to ignore the way he felt about Jazmyn. All week he'd had to avoid her in order to deal with her presence. "Give her time." Both Kirsten and Jason told him that. Well, how much time did he need to give her? How would he know she was ready?

Kirsten had told him about her lunch with Jazmyn. She said Jazmyn felt awful for being so angry with him, but she sure hadn't apologized. Maybe she thought she was justified. Then again, maybe she didn't want to encourage him, didn't feel for him what he felt for her.

After her teasing comment this morning he'd hoped they might at least become friends. Then he realized he didn't want to be just friends with her; he wanted to marry her and be with her the rest of his life.

In the truck he noticed how she tried her best not to touch him, even on the rough roads. It hurt to think she disliked him that much. Although he tried not to show it, he'd looked forward to her touch, even an impersonal one.

He crouched down again and motioned to Jason and Jazmyn. "Go over to that group of trees and wait. I'm going down over this ridge. It's a steep drop-off, but there's a cave down there that might be a good spot for a den. If they're there, I'll come and get you. Watch your step, though, it's almost straight down."

He waited until they were settled, then approached the ravine, keeping low. As he neared the edge, something flashed on the far side of the chasm. He eased out over the edge. A deer leaped up, racing full tilt out of the gorge, her breathing labored, blood running down her flank. Thor scrambled up, trying to get away. Something hit him hard in the side. Pain shot through him.

He must have blacked out. When he came to, he was lying at an odd angle, his side throbbing. He touched his shirt. Something sticky covered his fingers. Blood. He closed his eyes, letting darkness wash over him.

"Thor. O God, please let him be alive." Soft fingers touched his face. Thor didn't want to open his eyes. He was afraid he was hallucinating, thinking Jazmyn cared enough to be here to help him. She would never climb down such a steep slope.

The fingers brushed his hair back, flicked pieces of debris from his face. He forced his eyes to crack open. The dream Jazmyn looked very real. Tears made her eyes a bright, glittery green. She leaned over and kissed him on the forehead. Her lips were warm and soft like real lips. This was a dream he didn't want to end. He closed his eyes.

"Thor, you have to look at me." Jazmyn's breath warmed his cheek.

His eyes opened again. She was still there, still as beautiful as ever, and crying over him. If he could move, he would pull her to him and give her a long kiss.

"That would be wonderful." Jazmyn smiled at him. Thor realized he must have spoken the thought out loud. "I don't think you're up to the grabbing, but I can help out in the kissing department."

He almost forgot the pain in his body as she covered his mouth with hers. It was the sweetest kiss he could ever remember, and the most meaningful.

"Now we need to get down to business." Jazmyn lifted his first-aid kit. She must have brought it from the truck. "Jason took off to get help. I get to play doctor."

Her fingers trembled as she opened his shirt. "We saw what

happened. Some hunters must have been after that deer. They shot at her, but you were in the way. They got you instead."

"I'm not sure I'll taste as good." Thor winced as she tugged the shirt away from his side.

"I'm sorry." Tears pooled in her eyes. "I'm trying to be gentle."

"You're the best doctor I've ever had." He forced a smile. He managed to take her hand and lift it to his lips. His kiss brought a flush of color to her cheeks. "I love you, Jazmyn. I always will." A single tear tracked down her cheek. "I know I hurt you, but I didn't mean to. You don't have to return my love; I just had to tell you."

He closed his eyes and let her hand drop. He heard her start to sob. Something soft touched his cheek, again and again. She was kissing him. He opened his eyes.

Her green gaze caught his. "I love you so much, Thor Larson. If you think I'm going to let you say you love me and then watch you die, you're crazy. You will live through this. Understand?" Her white face had a determined look.

"As you wish, my lady."

"I know this will hurt, but I need to check your wound. I'm thinking you might have broken some bones in the fall, too, so I don't want to move you."

He gritted his teeth and held his breath as she worked the material free of the wound. Darkness closed in, but he heard her voice. He clung to the sound. "This doesn't look at all bad. I'm going to try to cover this with some gauze and tape it down. I'm hoping that will stop the bleeding."

Time passed in a haze. A shout sounded from above. The steady beat of helicopter rotors drew near. Someone other than Jazmyn was now leaning over him, examining him.

"Thor, can you hear me?"

He opened his eyes. Jazmyn leaned close. He wanted to tell

her how beautiful she was, but his mouth didn't work.

"The rescue team is here. They're going to put you in a basket and get you to the helicopter. You've lost a lot of blood. They think you have some broken ribs, a broken leg, and a concussion. I'll see you at the hospital. Jason will bring me."

She leaned over. Her kiss was so sweet. "I love you, Thor. Now and always."

He couldn't quit smiling as they loaded him onto the stretcher and hoisted him into the air.

epilogue

Thor watched Jazmyn as he ended his phone conversation. The windows were wide open, letting in a fresh fall breeze. She stood on a platform he'd built for her. In one hand she held a sponge, in the other a palette of paint. She was putting the finishing touches on a woodland scene along one wall of the nursery.

"Was that Wes?" Jazmyn didn't look away from her work. She must have heard him set down the phone.

"Yep. The new father. Kirsten and Wes have a new baby boy."

Jazmyn turned to him, her face shining. "How soon can we go see him?"

"Whoa, there." He reached her in three long strides. "Be careful. Just because the scaffold is safe doesn't mean you can't fall off." He swung her down.

Taking the painting equipment from her hands, he pulled her into his arms for a long kiss. When he stopped, she was as breathless as he was.

All around him the walls were covered with scenes of the forest. "Do you know what happens when you're surrounded by forest? You run the risk of being attacked by a wild animal."

Jazmyn laughed. "The problem is my wild animal has turned into a tame husband." Her arms snaked up to wrap around his neck. "Maybe I'm the one becoming wild."

"Only when I bring out the chocolate. Then I can see traces

of Xena in you." Thor gave his wife another kiss.

"That's because I'm craving it and can't have it," she pouted.

He nibbled at her lower lip. "I'm trying to help you out. I've been eating plenty of chocolate for you."

"You're awful." She gave him another kiss. "I should get out of here and let the paint dry. Let's see if Erik's heard about the baby."

Thor closed the windows. Taking her hand, he paused to look around the room. Jazmyn had done a remarkable job of making the nursery feel like the outdoors.

"Kirsten and Wes may have had their baby before us, but ours will have the best bedroom."

"Are you sure you don't mind living in town now?" Jazmyn gazed up at him, concern evident in her green eyes.

He took a deep breath. "No. Kirsten will need me to step in while she's with the baby. As long as we can get away once in a while to the cabin, I don't mind at all. How about you?"

"I can be content anywhere you are, Thor. You know that, don't you?"

Pulling her close, Thor rested his chin on her head. The lump in his throat kept him quiet. A year had passed since he'd been hurt in the mountains. Jazmyn had been with him every step of the way while he healed. Six months ago, they'd married and moved up to his cabin in the mountains. She hadn't complained once, until the day he told her they would have to move back to town for a while.

If he had any doubts about the sincerity of her love, he could look at the changes in her. She was the one who insisted their child would live in the forest no matter where they were. She'd taken him on a shopping spree when they got to town. Stuffed toys placed around the baby's room represented all the wild animals from the mountains.

They continued down the stairs. Thor didn't think he could be more content than he was now. They may have rough times ahead, but he knew their faith and love would see them through.

A Letter To Our Readers

Dear Reader:

In order that we might better contribute to your reading enjoyment, we would appreciate your taking a few minutes to respond to the following questions. We welcome your comments and read each form and letter we receive. When completed, please return to the following:

Fiction Editor
Heartsong Presents
PO Box 719
Uhrichsville, Ohio 44683

1. Did you enjoy reading *Picture Imperfect* by Nancy J. Farrier?
   ❑ Very much! I would like to see more books by this author!
   ❑ Moderately. I would have enjoyed it more if

   _____

   _____

   _____

2. Are you a member of **Heartsong Presents**? ❑ Yes ❑ No
   If no, where did you purchase this book? _____

   _____

3. How would you rate, on a scale from 1 (poor) to 5 (superior), the cover design? _____

4. On a scale from 1 (poor) to 10 (superior), please rate the following elements.

   ____ Heroine   ____ Plot
   ____ Hero   ____ Inspirational theme
   ____ Setting   ____ Secondary characters

5. These characters were special because?_____

_____

_____

6. How has this book inspired your life?_____

_____

_____

7. What settings would you like to see covered in future
   Heartsong Presents books? _____

_____

_____

8. What are some inspirational themes you would like to see
   treated in future books? _____

_____

_____

9. Would you be interested in reading other **Heartsong
   Presents** titles? ❏ Yes ❏ No

10. Please check your age range:
   ❏ Under 18 ❏ 18-24
   ❏ 25-34 ❏ 35-45
   ❏ 46-55 ❏ Over 55

Name_____

Occupation _____

Address _____

City_____ State_____ Zip_____

Sweet Treats

4 stories in 1

*T*hese four complete novels follow the culinary adventures—and misadventures—of Cynthia and three of her culinary students who want to stir up a little romance.

Four seasoned authors blend their skills in this delightful compilation: Wanda E. Brunstetter, Birdie L. Etchison, Pamela Griffin, and Tamela Hancock Murray.

Contemporary, paperback, 368 pages, 5 ³/₁₆" x 8"

❤ ❤ ❤ ❤ ❤ ❤ ❤ ❤ ❤ ❤ ❤ ❤ ❤ ❤ ❤ ❤

Please send me _____ copies of *Sweet Treats.* I am enclosing $6.97 for each. (Please add $2.00 to cover postage and handling per order. OH add 7% tax.)

Send check or money order, no cash or C.O.D.s please.

Name _____

Address _____

City, State, Zip _____

To place a credit card order, call 1-800-847-8270.
Send to: Heartsong Presents Reader Service, PO Box 721, Uhrichsville, OH 44683

❤ ❤ ❤ ❤ ❤ ❤ ❤ ❤ ❤ ❤ ❤ ❤ ❤ ❤ ❤ ❤

Heartsong

Any 12 Heartsong Presents titles for only $27.00*

CONTEMPORARY ROMANCE IS CHEAPER BY THE DOZEN!

Buy any assortment of twelve *Heartsong Presents* titles and save 25% off of the already discounted price of $2.97 each!

*plus $2.00 shipping and handling per order and sales tax where applicable.

HEARTSONG PRESENTS TITLES AVAILABLE NOW:

___HP242 *Far Above Rubies*, B. Melby & C. Wienke
___HP245 *Crossroads*, T. and J. Peterson
___HP246 *Brianna's Pardon*, G. Clover
___HP261 *Race of Love*, M. Panagiotopoulos
___HP262 *Heaven's Child*, G. Fields
___HP265 *Hearth of Fire*, C. L. Reece
___HP278 *Elizabeth's Choice*, L. Lyle
___HP298 *A Sense of Belonging*, T. Fowler
___HP302 *Seasons*, G. G. Martin
___HP305 *Call of the Mountain*, Y. Lehman
___HP306 *Piano Lessons*, G. Sattler
___HP317 *Love Remembered*, A. Bell
___HP318 *Born for This Love*, B. Bancroft
___HP321 *Fortress of Love*, M. Panagiotopoulos
___HP322 *Country Charm*, D. Mills
___HP325 *Gone Camping*, G. Sattler
___HP326 *A Tender Melody*, B. L. Etchison
___HP329 *Meet My Sister, Tess*, K. Billerbeck
___HP330 *Dreaming of Castles*, G. G. Martin
___HP337 *Ozark Sunrise*, H. Alexander
___HP338 *Somewhere a Rainbow*, Y. Lehman
___HP341 *It Only Takes a Spark*, P. K. Tracy
___HP342 *The Haven of Rest*, A. Boeshaar
___HP349 *Wild Tiger Wind*, G. Buck
___HP350 *Race for the Roses*, L. Snelling
___HP353 *Ice Castle*, J. Livingston
___HP354 *Finding Courtney*, B. L. Etchison
___HP361 *The Name Game*, M. G. Chapman
___HP377 *Come Home to My Heart*, J. A. Grote
___HP378 *The Landlord Takes a Bride*, K. Billerbeck
___HP390 *Love Abounds*, A. Bell
___HP394 *Equestrian Charm*, D. Mills
___HP401 *Castle in the Clouds*, A. Boeshaar
___HP402 *Secret Ballot*, Y. Lehman
___HP405 *The Wife Degree*, A. Ford
___HP406 *Almost Twins*, G. Sattler
___HP409 *A Living Soul*, H. Alexander
___HP410 *The Color of Love*, D. Mills
___HP413 *Remnant of Victory*, J. Odell

___HP414 *The Sea Beckons*, B. L. Etchison
___HP417 *From Russia with Love*, C. Coble
___HP418 *Yesteryear*, G. Brandt
___HP421 *Looking for a Miracle*, W. E. Brunstetter
___HP422 *Condo Mania*, M. G. Chapman
___HP425 *Mustering Courage*, L. A. Coleman
___HP426 *To the Extreme*, T. Davis
___HP429 *Love Ahoy*, C. Coble
___HP430 *Good Things Come*, J. A. Ryan
___HP433 *A Few Flowers*, G. Sattler
___HP434 *Family Circle*, J. L. Barton
___HP438 *Out in the Real World*, K. Paul
___HP441 *Cassidy's Charm*, D. Mills
___HP442 *Vision of Hope*, M. H. Flinkman
___HP445 *McMillian's Matchmakers*, G. Sattler
___HP449 *An Ostrich a Day*, N. J. Farrier
___HP450 *Love in Pursuit*, D. Mills
___HP454 *Grace in Action*, K. Billerbeck
___HP458 *The Candy Cane Calaboose*, J. Spaeth
___HP461 *Pride and Pumpernickel*, A. Ford
___HP462 *Secrets Within*, G. G. Martin
___HP465 *Talking for Two*, W. E. Brunstetter
___HP466 *Risa's Rainbow*, A. Boeshaar
___HP469 *Beacon of Truth*, P. Griffin
*___HP470 *Carolina Pride*, T. Fowler
___HP473 *The Wedding's On*, G. Sattler
___HP474 *You Can't Buy Love*, K. Y'Barbo
___HP477 *Extreme Grace*, T. Davis
___HP478 *Plain and Fancy*, W. E. Brunstetter
___HP481 *Unexpected Delivery*, C. M. Hake
___HP482 *Hand Quilted with Love*, J. Livingston
___HP485 *Ring of Hope*, B. L. Etchison
___HP486 *The Hope Chest*, W. E. Brunstetter
___HP489 *Over Her Head*, G. G. Martin
___HP490 *A Class of Her Own*, J. Thompson
___HP493 *Her Home or Her Heart*, K. Elaine
___HP494 *Mended Wheels*, A. Bell & J. Sagal
___HP497 *Flames of Deceit*, R. Dow & A. Snaden

(If ordering from this page, please remember to include it with the order form.)

Presents

___HP498 *Charade*, P. Humphrey	___HP554 *A Donut a Day*, G. Sattler
___HP501 *The Thrill of the Hunt*, T. H. Murray	___HP557 *If You Please*, T. Davis
___HP502 *Whole in One*, A. Ford	___HP558 *A Fairy Tale Romance*,
___HP505 *Happily Ever After*,	M. Panagiotopoulos
M. Panagiotopoulos	___HP561 *Ton's Vow*, K. Cornelius
___HP506 *Cords of Love*, L. A. Coleman	___HP562 *Family Ties*, J. L. Barton
___HP509 *His Christmas Angel*, G. Sattler	___HP565 *An Unbreakable Hope*, K. Billerbeck
___HP510 *Past the Ps Please*, Y. Lehman	___HP566 *The Baby Quilt*, J. Livingston
___HP513 *Licorice Kisses*, D. Mills	___HP569 *Ageless Love*, L. Bliss
___HP514 *Roger's Return*, M. Davis	___HP570 *Beguiling Masquerade*, C. G. Page
___HP517 *The Neighborly Thing to Do*,	___HP573 *In a Land Far Far Away*,
W. E. Brunstetter	M. Panagiotopoulos
___HP518 *For a Father's Love*, J. A. Grote	___HP574 *Lambert's Pride*, L. A. Coleman and
___HP521 *Be My Valentine*, J. Livingston	R. Hauck
___HP522 *Angel's Roost*, J. Spaeth	___HP577 *Anita's Fortune*, K. Cornelius
___HP525 *Game of Pretend*, J. Odell	___HP578 *The Birthday Wish*, J. Livingston
___HP526 *In Search of Love*, C. Lynxwiler	___HP581 *Love Online*, K. Billerbeck
___HP529 *Major League Dad*, K. Y'Barbo	___HP582 *The Long Ride Home*, A. Boeshaar
___HP530 *Joe's Diner*, G. Sattler	___HP585 *Compassion's Charm*, D. Mills
___HP533 *On a Clear Day*, Y. Lehman	___HP586 *A Single Rose*, P. Griffin
___HP534 *Term of Love*, M. Pittman Crane	___HP589 *Changing Seasons*, C. Reece and
___HP537 *Close Enough to Perfect*, T. Fowler	J. Reece-Demarco
___HP538 *A Storybook Finish*, L. Bliss	___HP590 *Secret Admirer*, G. Sattler
___HP541 *The Summer Girl*, A. Boeshaar	___HP593 *Angel Incognito*, J. Thompson
___HP542 *Clowning Around*, W. E. Brunstetter	___HP594 *Out on a Limb*, G. Gaymer Martin
___HP545 *Love Is Patient*, C. M. Hake	___HP597 *Let My Heart Go*, B. Huston
___HP546 *Love Is Kind*, J. Livingston	___HP598 *More Than Friends*, T. Hancock
___HP549 *Patchwork and Politics*, C. Lynxwiler	Murray
___HP550 *Woodhaven Acres*, B. Etchison	___HP601 *Timing is Everything*, T. V. Bateman
___HP553 *Bay Island*, B. Loughner	___HP602 *Dandelion Bride*, J. Livingston

Great Inspirational Romance at a Great Price!

Heartsong Presents books are inspirational romances in contemporary and historical settings, designed to give you an enjoyable, spirit-lifting reading experience. You can choose wonderfully written titles from some of today's best authors like Hannah Alexander, Andrea Boeshaar, Yvonne Lehman, Tracie Peterson, and many others.

When ordering quantities less than twelve, above titles are $2.97 each.
Not all titles may be available at time of order.

SEND TO: **Heartsong Presents** Reader's Service
              P.O. Box 721, Uhrichsville, Ohio 44683

Please send me the items checked above. I am enclosing $ _____
(please add $2.00 to cover postage per order. OH add 7% tax. NJ
add 6%.). Send check or money order, no cash or C.O.D.s, please.

To place a credit card order, call 1-800-847-8270.

NAME _____

ADDRESS _____

CITY/STATE _____ ZIP_____

HPS 10-04

_H_EARTSONG ❤ PRESENTS

Love Stories
Are Rated G!

That's for godly, gratifying, and of course, great! If you love a
thrilling love story but don't appreciate the sordidness of some
popular paperback romances, **Heartsong Presents** is for you. In
fact, **Heartsong Presents** is the premiere inspirational romance
book club featuring love stories where Christian faith is the primary
ingredient in a marriage relationship.

Sign up today to receive your first set of four, never-before-
published Christian romances. Send no money now; you will
receive a bill with the first shipment. You may cancel at any time
without obligation, and if you aren't completely satisfied with any
selection, you may return the books for an immediate refund!

Imagine. . .four new romances every four weeks—two historical,
two contemporary—with men and women like you who long to
meet the one God has chosen as the love of their lives. . .all for the
low price of $10.99 postpaid.

To join, simply complete the coupon below and mail to the
address provided. **Heartsong Presents** romances are rated G for
another reason: They'll arrive Godspeed!

YES! Sign me up for Hearts❤ng!

NEW MEMBERSHIPS WILL BE SHIPPED IMMEDIATELY!
Send no money now. We'll bill you only $10.99 post-
paid with your first shipment of four books. Or for faster
action, call toll free 1-800-847-8270.

NAME_____

ADDRESS_____

CITY_____STATE_____ ZIP_____

MAIL TO: HEARTSONG PRESENTS, P.O. Box 721, Uhrichsville, Ohio 44683
or visit www.heartsongpresents.com